Tubby Dubonnet mysteries by Tony Dunbar:

The Crime Czar

TONY DUNBAR

A Dell Book

Published by
Dell Publishing
a division of
Bantam Doubleday Dell Publishing Group, Inc.
1540 Broadway
New York, New York 10036

This novel is a work of fiction. Names, characters, places, and incidents either are the product of the author's imagination or are used fictitiously. Any resemblance to actual persons, living or dead, events, or locales is entirely coincidental. There is no Tubby Dubonnet and the real New Orleans is different from his make-believe city.

The trademark Dell® is registered in the U.S. Patent and Trademark Office.

ISBN: 0-440-22658-9

Printed in the United States of America

Published simultaneously in Canada

November 1998

10 9 8 7 6 5 4 3 2 1

WCD

To Sam, Sam,
the working man.

I gratefully acknowledge the thoughtful comments of Hugh Knox and Linda Kravitz, the tavern of Ned Hobgood, and the coffee of Theone Perloff-Velez.

1

The red glow from the stoplight wrapped around Daisy like a bloody veil. She leaned against the crooked bus-stop sign on Airline Highway, fighting the craving for a cigarette. Crimson nighttime mist swirled about her face. It was warm, almost midnight. She listened for the low mournful horns of the boats on the Mississippi River a mile away and traveled with them down a dark twisting channel in her mind. Her skirt was hiked up high on her thigh. She was working.

The headlamps of the cars driving out of New Orleans became visible when they were still a great distance away. Daisy watched them bear down, and if the light was green, roar past her. The four-lane highway ran straight as an arrow pointed west. It shot past cheap motels and all-night gas stations, then sailed through open marsh and prairie all the way to Baton Rouge. Seeing the lights come, Daisy had time to imagine who might be behind the wheel of this car or that, compose her face, straighten her tired back, and cast what she believed was an inviting look at the dark windshields. She kept one leg forward, displayed on tiptoe, in the belief that that was where men's eyes focused first. Shadowy heads suddenly materialized behind the glass, and she caught glimpses of faces, but unless someone saw her look, pressed the brake pedal, and rolled the window down, the occupant could have been a movie star or a werewolf for all she knew.

It was an underrated talent, she thought, being able to pose like this in cowgirl boots, big hair in place, smelling good, lipstick fresh, unaffected by semis grinding through their gears and the toot-toot of strangers' horns. Daisy never had to wait long.

Shortly, some pipeline worker or shipfitter would slow down. The car or the pickup truck would swerve a little bit to check her out in the headlights. She might hear the motor purring and the tires squeak. There would be that moment of suspense, while those ship horns sounded in the distance, until the passenger window slid away, when she could finally see who was in there, who was sizing her up.

Then with a shrug of her bare shoulders, she would push off the bus-stop sign, take a step forward, and bend down to show what cleavage she could compress out of her purple vest embroidered with black cats and blue moons.

"How ya doin'?" was Daisy's icebreaker, if the guy was grinning or drooling too much to think of anything to say. They could usually take it from there. Drive around the block and park. Twenty minutes later, or an hour, depending, she'd be back at the bus stop again.

Daisy felt the wind blow around her legs and lift her skirt. A pickup truck with chrome pipes sticking out above the cab raced by. The boys inside screamed naughty words at her as the engine backfired. She had seen them drive by before—they were too chicken to stop. Daisy flipped them the bird, which they probably couldn't see. Anybody got too fresh, she kept a can of Mace in her boot, the working girl's friend.

The lights from a shopping center blazed in the distance. Crickets chirped lazily in the weeds that fought for life through the holes in the sidewalk. On other nights, when it wasn't so foggy, she could see the glow of downtown New Orleans in the east—somewhere above the point where the black highway met the night sky.

A car roared by like a jet taking off, and she had to reach up with both hands to hold her hair.

"Damn," she fussed, and failed to notice the pickup truck cruising slowly, real close to the curb, until it was almost upon her.

2

Only the guys with shaggy hair and scars on their faces and the girls with the sequined skirts and stars in their eyes remained this late at the Temple of Love Karaoke Bar on Chef Menteur Highway. The last of the paying customers had gone off into the night, tires screeching and CD-players blasting, and Singh Phi Lo was counting out his dough in the back office. His girls, Binh Ho and Oyster Lady, finished their drinks and smokes at the bar, freshened their perfume, and prepared to split. The lonely stretch of reclaimed swamp alongside the Intracoastal Waterway, known to some as Little Saigon, closed up early.

Singh's son, Xuan, and two of his buddies were hanging around in the parking lot outside. They were shooting the breeze about how much it would cost to put a custom paint job, with pictures of shrimp boats and leaping dolphins and stuff like that, on Xuan's van. They were all stoned and past drunk and not taking any shit off anybody. The blinking neon sign above the club provided the only light. There was so little traffic on the road that you could hear the lonely ship horns on the waterway and a baby whimpering in a trailer out back.

Xuan saw a nice-looking Plymouth Talon sail past, heading east toward the wilderness of Bayou Sauvage. He noted that it slowed suddenly and pulled off into the drive of an abandoned motel a hundred yards down the highway, but this did not interrupt his train of thought about dolphins.

The Plymouth made a deliberate U-turn, and the headlights lurched back onto the highway. The car's return got Xuan's full attention, and he flicked his cigarette in that direction to alert his friends. The little red coal bounced when it hit the asphalt and then lay still.

The Plymouth switched on its high beams and cruised slowly toward the bar. Xuan was checking his pockets for his Marlboros when the side of the vehicle came alive with an earsplitting din and bright orange flames and the back of his head blew off. Running from the searing light and deafening hammering of the guns, his two partners were cut down, and they slammed into the pavement squirming. The Plymouth stopped, and the gunmen inside carefully finished the job, blasting the crawling forms until they were motionless and smashing the painted windows of the tavern. The Temple of Love sign exploded, and a burglar alarm was screaming somewhere inside, demanding help that would not come.

Satisfied, the Plymouth's driver hit the accelerator, and the car shot down the dark highway toward New Orleans. While the moaning women inside huddled under a cocktail table, Singh Phi Lo crawled out the back fire door, his military .45 clutched in his fist. He pulled himself on his elbows through the oyster shells and broken pop bottles that covered the ground to the corner of the building. He was in time to see a car's taillights disappear in the distance. Then he saw the mess in the parking lot that had been his son. The burglar alarm wound down and in the trailer out back the baby's wails joined his own.

3

"Shit!" Daisy exclaimed when she spotted the pickup truck nearly upon her. She took a small hop backward. One heel caught in the uneven sidewalk and she almost fell.

The truck stopped, and she wiped the loose hairs off her forehead, trying to regain her poise.

"Hey, Daisy." It was a deep male voice.

"Oh, it's the weirdo," she said, recovering. She leaned over to peer inside the window. "Looks like you got your hair cut."

The man inside, whose name was Charlie Autin, grinned and took one hand off the wheel to pat his sideburns.

"Yeah, I'm cleaning up."

The light changed to green. An old junker dragging its muffler beeped and rattled past in the center lane, but Charlie stayed where he was.

"Nice night," he said pleasantly.

"You want to have some fun?" She put on her wicked smile.

"Sure. My name's Charlie, in case you forgot."

"Sure, Charlie." She popped open the door. The truck, bright white in the daytime, had turned a disturbing lime sherbet under the traffic light. She climbed in, and her skirt rode up so high in the process that Charlie's eyes turned into moons.

"What's the program?" Daisy asked, bouncing onto the seat. She swung around to give her customer the full-court view.

"Uh, same as last time. That was real nice."

"Hadn't you better move the truck?" she suggested.

"Right." He jammed the shifter into gear. The light had turned red again by then, but Charlie ran it anyway.

He wasn't so hard to look at—a strong jaw and big brown eyes were his best features. And he was built okay, too. At least she remembered that much from last time. Most of her customers were losers—old coots, smelly fat men, stuff like that. Of course, she hadn't really been at this forever. It was just something she was doing to make ends meet while she got her life back together.

"You been here long?" he asked.

"Couple of hours, maybe. Why?"

"No, I didn't mean that," he said, turning at the next corner. "Are you, like, from around here?"

"The life story is extra, weirdo. You got a cigarette?"

"No," he said, hurt. "I don't smoke. You want to go to Circle K? I'll buy you a pack."

Daisy checked her hair in the mirror.

"No," she said. "I got some in my apartment." She bit her lip. "I mean, at the motel." She didn't want her customers to know she actually lived in the little room at the Tomcat Inn. She didn't want any surprise visits from the old geezers.

"I grew up on the river in Luling," he said. "Ever been there?"

"Never heard of it," she said, staring out the window at the hardware store they were passing. The red signs were pushing Roach Prufe. She had only been in New Orleans a little over a month, and she knew where the river was only because one of the jerks had insisted on doing it on the levee instead of in her bed at the motel. She had gotten eaten up by mosquitoes in very private places and did not plan to go back.

Her room was clean, and Bronstein, the manager, would come to her rescue in a flash if he knew she was in trouble. They had an arrangement that involved an extra twenty bucks a day and a hand job on Sunday mornings when Mrs. Bronstein was in church. He was so grateful she felt like a nurse.

Charlie curb-jumped into the Tomcat Inn parking lot and slammed over the speed bump, just like everybody did.

"Yo!" she yelled, almost bouncing into the roof of the cab.

Charlie jerked to a halt and got them parked while she dug her plastic key out of her magical vest.

Three steps and she had it in the door. The interior smelled like potpourri air freshener. If you didn't like it, too bad.

Charlie stepped lively. Daisy closed the door behind him and slipped on the chain. Usually she left it off, to facilitate a hasty exit if circumstances required, but she was beginning to feel comfortable around Charlie.

She sat down on the bed and began taking off her vest. Underneath she wore a red chemise with CAJUN FEST printed on it. That came off next, then the black Wonder Bra. Charlie sat beside her studying the process, hands clasped between his knees.

"You like what you're looking at, weirdo?" she asked. She turned to face him, not letting her hair flounce more than she could help it.

He nodded vigorously, his eyes focused below her chin.

"Well, give me your money," she said.

"Oh, sure." With difficulty Charlie dug a fat black wallet out of the back pocket of his jeans. He already had the bills counted, folded neatly, and stuck into one corner so he would be sure not to spend them on something else. Daisy double-checked his math quickly and poked the wad between the mattress and box spring.

"I guess you want the works," she said.

He put his hand on her breast and kept it there.

"I really like you, Daisy," he said, while she unbuttoned his shirt.

It gave her a good feeling to hear him say that, even though she figured it was just his body heat talking. He had plenty of that, her busy fingers quickly discovered.

Later on, Daisy let him take a shower, because he had been nice and because she had kind of enjoyed it. Then he was gone. He said he was going to show up in the morning and take her out for breakfast, but she blew him off. Another weirdo in her life, she didn't need. He was probably just bullshitting anyway. Daisy cleaned herself up, mailed herself a kiss in the mirror, and hit the streets.

4

ubby Dubonnet had read nearly every magazine in the waiting room. Three hours earlier he had been fresh out of bed, tying a knot in his Tabasco tie and getting ready to go to the office, when his youngest daughter, Collette, called excitedly to report that her sister was deep into labor. She was ready to deliver a baby at any moment.

The lawyer had hurried down to Touro Hospital to find that Debbie was installed in what they called a "birthing room." It was crowded to overflowing. The victim, in dim surroundings, was moaning in agony, attended by a nurse, a somewhat confused-looking doctor, and Tubby's ex-wife, Mattie, who was shouting at everyone. Marcos, whom Tubby still had difficulty considering Debbie's husband, was kneeling on the floor

beside the bed, apparently trying to induce a trance by
counting backward from a hundred. Tubby's other two
daughters, Collette and Christine, had been exiled to
the waiting room, and he hastily withdrew to join them.

There he learned that Debbie's labor had been going
on for most of the night but no one had thought to call
him. He stuffed his large frame into an armchair and re-
treated behind a *Newsweek* in a huff. In truth, however,
he did not regret that he had missed the chance to spend
the night cramped in a hospital room while his former
wife told everybody what to do.

The contractions dragged on for a couple more hours
anyhow, and Tubby or one of the girls would periodically
wander down the hall to check on Debbie's progress.
A nice white-haired lady arrived at around nine-thirty and
made a big pot of coffee. She offered everybody a cup.
Tubby struck up a conversation with a pipeline worker
from Buras who was also waiting for his daughter to give
birth. The guy was Tubby's age and had biceps like vol-
leyballs. Tubby had some muscles, too. He flexed them to
be sure.

"My first grandchild," Tubby told him.

"Me, it's my tenth," the guy boasted.

"Almost enough for a football team," Tubby joked.

"Yeah, I told my wife I'm gonna take 'em to the
Superdome an' see can they whip the Saints."

"It's a boy!" Christine cried, skipping down the hall.
They all hurried to the nursery to see the little red ball
arrive.

It was a stirring moment. It made the grandfather feel

like doing some push-ups. Maybe even a couple of cartwheels.

Later, Tubby was allowed to see Debbie long enough to tell her she had done well. The poor girl was beat and drifting in and out of sleep. Tubby shook Marcos's hand enthusiastically and told the new father to take good care of that child. "I will, Mr. Tubby," Marcos said, and there was something in his voice that made it sound like he might actually be up to the challenge. I hope you do a better job than I have, Tubby thought to himself, but he didn't really mean it. Right now he felt he might have done okay.

Walking to the elevator, he thought back to Debbie's wedding five months before. She had been a bit oversize walking down the aisle but had a good humor about it. The minister, who had pastored the Dubonnet flock for about twenty years, took it all in stride. He even accommodated the bride's special request that a second preacher— some guy she liked who ran a homeless shelter over in Mississippi—conduct part of the service. Tubby had never met the new young reverend, who had the improbable name of Buddy Holly, before the rehearsal, and he was not impressed by the sandy blond hair and wrinkled blue jeans. The Reverend Holly redeemed himself on the big day, however, by wearing a proper robe and by gripping Marcos tightly by the elbow just when the groom seemed in danger of tipping over backward into the flower array. Plus, in marked contrast to everyone else involved in the elaborate production, Buddy Holly said he did weddings for free.

Zoot-suited in a tux, Tubby had marched down the aisle proudly and given away the bride. He had played his part without a hitch, though he wanted to blubber when the bride said, "I do." It was only after the reception was winding down and Marcos and Debbie had slipped off to a hotel in the French Quarter that he had withdrawn into a corner by himself, clutching a glass of bourbon, and tried to imagine that his daughter had grown up and flown away.

Now it had all worked out fine.

Before leaving the hospital Tubby rode the elevator up to the next floor to check on another patient. His old friend Dan Haywood was in sad shape—felled by a bullet to the stomach when he inadvertently intervened in a bank heist during the past Mardi Gras. At first it had seemed that all would be well. There had even been moments when Dan returned to consciousness and been lucid enough to speak, though his words made little sense. But then some infection set in and the doctors talked about nerve damage before scurrying away to examine things they understood better.

Hacking sounds were coming from within Room G-13. Tubby rushed in to find that they were issuing from the other patient there, a frail old man with wisps of white hair on his yellow scalp, affliction unknown.

"Excuse me," Tubby mumbled, stepping around the curtain to Dan's side of the room.

His friend's head lay in the center of a crisp white pillow, as if it might not have moved for a long time, and his eyes were closed. Slow breathing lifted the blue blanket,

but the once-magnificent chest seemed now much reduced. Tubby pushed aside the tubes that dangled like
spaghetti around the massive head and shook Dan's
shoulder. He got a little grunt, not much but something.

"How's it going, buddy?" Tubby asked cheerfully, not
expecting any response. "They treating you all right?"

The man in the next bed hacked some more.

"Debbie just had a baby boy," Tubby rambled on. He
pushed a hand through his blond hair. "The little thing is
happy and healthy and nine pounds, and looks just like
our old wrestling coach. You remember Coach Ruggs?"

At a loss for more words, Tubby checked the IV bottles as if he knew what he was looking at.

"Anyway, we need you back, man. This old town
ain't the same without you."

"I knew him from the old neighborhood," Dan said
distinctly.

"What?" Tubby shouted, unwilling to trust his ears.
"Dan, what did you say? What did you say? Come on,
man." Frantically he shook the patient's shoulder while
grabbing for the nurse's call button.

"Come quick! He's speaking!" Tubby yelled into the
plastic mouthpiece. "Yeah, Dan, this is Tubby, from
the old neighborhood."

His friend's head tossed from side to side. Then he
exhaled deeply and lay still.

A nurse flew into the room, wanting to know what
had happened.

"He just spoke to me," Tubby reported excitedly.

But those words were Dan's entire speech for the day.

The nurse counted his pulse, adjusted a valve on one of the tubes, and said she would let the doctor know.

Tubby waited around hopefully and watched Dan's eyelids quiver.

The man who had shot Dan was called "Roux," or something like that, and he was supposed to be dead. Tubby had been there when the son of a bitch had blasted a hole in Dan's chest, and he had chased Roux through half the French Quarter before the gangster had escaped. A day or two later they had found what they believed was Roux's body, burned up in a campfire in the hobo jungle beside the Mississippi River. There was no doubt in Tubby's mind that Roux worked for someone yet to be identified. The obsession to track down that evil being had once burned hot and deep inside Tubby. A few months had passed, however, and he had succumbed to the prevailing view that some things in New Orleans were beyond anybody's control. The difficulty was, of course, that he found that conclusion depressing.

Outside on the sidewalk the day was hot, despite the black clouds rolling low over the magnolias and live oaks that shaded Prytania Street. Tubby had been prepared to face up to his office routine when he first got out of bed, but the birth of a grandson and the encouraging visit to Dan had given the morning a new slant. Seeing this was such a special day, he thought he might just drive over to Mike's Bar and hoist a few. Strange thing was, he had been doing that a lot lately, and not all of his days were special.

5

harlie Autin actually showed up at the Tomcat Inn for breakfast. Since he knew what Daisy did for a living, he waited until after ten o'clock before he came tapping on her door, and even then he half expected to have to beat a hasty retreat if she was mad or had someone with her. He couldn't get her out of his mind. She wasn't the kind of girl his mom would want him to bring home, but mom was in jail, anyway. Charlie had a suspicion, however, that whoring around was only a temporary situation for Daisy. Sex with her had his brain wound up so tightly that he was overwhelmed by embarrassing sensations of pleasure, but it was more than that. He could tell that this was a girl with a lot of heart.

"Who is it?" she shouted.

"Uh, Charlie," he said, addressing the chipped door. "You know, breakfast."

"Oh, shit," he heard her say. There was some banging around before the door crashed open. She was in a blue robe and squinted at him with one hand shading her eyes from the bright morning sunshine.

"The weirdo," she stated flatly. A few strands of hair escaped from the shiny pink scarf she had loosely tied around her head.

Charlie put on his best smile. Daisy didn't look so exotic right after she woke up in the morning, but that made her no less alluring in his eyes.

"I thought you might want some eggs. Or ham, maybe," he said.

"You did." She sized him up. He wasn't bad-looking if you didn't mind eyes spaced too far apart and hair that stuck out like a wildberry bush. Daisy started to giggle.

Charlie blushed and stepped back, prepared to give it up.

"I'm sorry . . . ," he began.

"Hell, I guess I've got to eat so I might as well let you pay for it," she said and almost laughed again at the way his slightly undernourished face lit up.

"Go wait in the truck," she directed and closed the door in Charlie's face.

He socked his fists into his palms, adjusted his pants, and hastened to his pickup to dust off the passenger seat.

She made him wait about twenty-five minutes, but she came out fresh and clean wearing a pair of black jeans and a creamy sleeveless top. She looked a lot like the girl who had refused to go with Charlie to the high school prom on account of they would not let him graduate.

He held the door for her and would have helped her climb up if she hadn't moved so fast.

"Where to?" she asked when he got in beside her.

"I was thinking Denny's," he said.

"Fine with me," she said, impressed that he was going first-class. "They got biscuits and gravy."

Charlie drove onto the Causeway. They didn't talk, but he watched her out of the corner of his eye. She caught him once and frowned at him. That got him smiling, and he started humming "You Are My Sunshine." She rolled her eyes and looked out the window at the endless panorama of strip shopping centers, muffler shops, and gas stations they were passing.

At Denny's the air conditioner was set so high she began shivering. So Charlie sat right next to her in the booth and put his arm around her shoulder. She let him, just as if they were on a real date.

Daisy ordered biscuits and gravy and three eggs, over-easy, and hash browns and grits and bacon and sausage and orange juice and coffee. Charlie had the number five.

"So, how long you been here?" he asked.

"I told you not to ask for my life story."

"Well, it would be nice to know something about you, other than . . ."

She looked at him sharply.

"Well, you know. Something normal," he concluded.

She took a big gulp of coffee.

"I've been here nearly two months. I came on the bus from Loxley, Alabama. Does that tell you anything?"

"Sure, that's a start."

"I don't know how normal it is, though," she said, reaching for the cream pitcher.

"I paint cars for a living," Charlie said.

"That's nice."

"But I'm looking around for a better job."

She snorted.

"I believe everybody can change the way they are." He studied his knuckles.

She shot a glance at his profile and thought of several cute things to say.

"I don't guess it hurts anything to believe that," she said instead.

"Yeah, I figure we've all got to have a bright picture of where we want to go in our minds, if we ever want to get there."

The waitress showed up and spread plates of food all over the table.

"You're weird," Daisy said, shaking pepper on her eggs until they were mostly black. "I like eggs with my pepper," she commented.

"Maybe I am weird," Charlie said and took his arm from around her shoulder so he could grab a fork.

"Biscuits were better back home," she said reflectively.

"They got Denny's there, too?" Charlie asked.

Too weird, Daisy thought, and patted his thigh.

6

Tubby rolled into his office a little after two o'clock. Circling the spiral ramp of the Place Palais parking garage, feeling three beers slosh around, he hoped that Cherrylynn, his secretary, was out for lunch. She had been the first to comment upon the progressive irregularity of his life. Except when the kids slept over, which wasn't often, Tubby lived alone. And since he had lost his law partner, Reggie Turntide, he worked alone, too. So hell, who else but his secretary would notice. All of Tubby's best friends were alcoholics. Some were drunks.

He locked the door of his not-yet-paid-for Chrysler Le Baron, squared his shoulders, and took the elevator to the forty-third floor. At the far end of the hall, the

gold letters that said DUBONNET & ASSOCIATES, ATTOR-
NEYS AT LAW beckoned him, and he fought the urge to
run away.

Cautiously, Tubby grasped the brass handle and
pushed open the tall walnut door.

"Good afternoon, Mr. Dubonnet," Cherrylynn said
lightly. There was no mistaking, however, the worry in
her eyes.

"Good afternoon," he replied. "Guess who's a grandfather."

"Ooh!" she squealed. All of her freckles danced.
"Debbie had her baby!"

"Yep," Tubby said proudly. "Nine pounds and it's
a boy."

"What's his name?"

"She hasn't decided yet."

"Everything is fine?"

"Oh, yeah. She's just worn out."

"What time did the baby come?" Cherrylynn wanted
all the details. Part of her function as Tubby's recep-
tionist, secretary, and let's face it, manager of his law
practice, was to try to get the whole picture.

"At about ten o'clock this morning," he told her before he recognized the trap.

His manager checked her watch.

"I had a meeting . . . to go to," he said and marched
toward his private office. "Any phone messages?"

"They're all arranged on your desk, boss." He knew
they would be. She was such a valuable person to have

around that he would have to put in a couple of hours work just so he could afford to pay her.

He looked warily around his office, waiting for the inevitable stress to set in. The familiar things—the worn cypress desk, the leather-upholstered chair, the pictures of his children—were comforting, but in this season he was weary of being a lawyer. He had felt that way ever since Dan got shot, since it had been driven home to him how casually lives could be thrown away—if they interfered with making big bucks in the Big Easy. It was not that he was naive. It was just that he was programmed to right the wrongs around him. This time he did not know how, and he wasn't coping very well with the frustration.

Tubby tossed his briefcase onto the desk and went to the window to squint through his red telescope. Ah, two ladies in colorful bikinis were sunning themselves beside the bright blue pool situated on the roof of the Fairmont Hotel. That could still get a rise out of him, so he must not be depressed, exactly, he thought while adjusting the knob. He was just pissed off at the whole damn city.

"Mr. Dubonnet." Cherrylynn was standing in the doorway. "Judge Hughes called this morning. He said it was important."

She was fretting, as if perhaps Tubby had missed a court date or forgotten to file a brief.

"Really?" Tubby took his eye away from the telescope. The day had cleared, and he could see the city stretching out below him from Lake Pontchartrain to the yellow-and-blue marshes past Chalmette. He had an eagle's eye view of the French Quarter, the sharp curve of the Mississippi where the river ate a channel six hundred feet deep, the last point of land at the Rigolets, and the endless water beyond.

"I'll call him right away." Tubby smiled at his secretary reassuringly, and she nodded and slipped away. She need not have worried about him messing up his docket. Never screw a client and never lie to the judge were still his guidelines. And, of late, he had been avoiding taking on clients with the kinds of problems he could screw up.

"Mrs. Evans, this is Tubby Dubonnet. May I speak to the judge?" Tubby was gingerly seated at his desk, flipping nervously through a thick pile of pink message slips.

"Counselor," Judge Hughes's voice boomed into his ear. "How are you today?"

"Fine, Judge. My daughter just had a baby."

He got to tell the story again.

"The Bible says 'Fruitful will be thy issue.' I feel this will be the first of many fine grandchildren for you."

"You could be right," Tubby said, trying to sound jovial. Christine was seventeen and Collette was fifteen, and he wasn't ready to think about either one of them getting pregnant just yet. Hell, Debbie had just turned twenty-one, but she had always been headstrong, and . . .

"I'll tell you why I called." The judge cut into his

reverie. "I want you to be the cochairman of my reelection campaign."

"What!" Tubby exclaimed. "Is it time for you to run again?"

"Every seven years I must go among the public, regular as a plague of locusts."

"Is anybody actually going to oppose you?"

"I've heard they will," the judge said, lowering his voice. "The one that I know of is Benny Bloom."

"Yeah?" Tubby could see where there might be a problem. Benny Bloom was a brash young attorney who ran spectacular ads on television where oil rigs caught fire and blew up. In the next scene, Benny is handing out checks to lots of smiling widows and guys wearing hard hats. He had all sorts of name recognition.

"Why would he want to be a judge? He'd have to take a huge cut in salary."

"That's what I can't figure out," Hughes said sourly. "He says he wants to pay the community back, some crap like that. I really don't know what his angle is."

"Well, I'll help you in any way that I can, Al, but what does a cochairman have to do? I've never been one before."

"Oh, you know, you sign your name to all my fund-raising letters, and you go to the rubber chicken dinners, and call all the right people. Nothing too strenuous."

"What about the fact that I'm white?"

The judge thought that was funny. "Hell, Tubby, I don't hold that against you. You remember the first time I ran, when you took me around and introduced me to all those high-class lawyers in the big firms downtown?"

"Sure."

"It helped me then. I want you to do the same thing this time, only on a different level. Anyway, my other cochairman is gonna be black."

"Who's that?"

"Reverend Horace Weems, only he doesn't know it yet. I'm gonna call him next."

"I don't believe I know the reverend."

"He pastors St. Pious the Third Evangelist Baptist on Orleans Avenue. He's a fine man. And listen, I've got a campaign manager, too, and I'm getting a media consultant. They're going to be doing all the nuts and bolts work."

"And me and the Reverend Weems?"

"You and the reverend are going to help me figure out how to pay for it all."

"I'm flattered, Al." And he was. "I could probably find the time." Since he didn't have any clients. "But as far as my personal financial contribution . . ."

Judge Hughes laughed so loud Tubby had to jerk the phone away from his ear.

"I don't need your money, Tubby," he roared. "I want you to help me get all those other lawyers' money."

Relieved, Tubby laughed with the judge. "Sure, Al," he said. "I'll be glad to do it."

"I knew you would. Either I or Mrs. Evans will call you in a day or two and set up a first campaign meeting."

"So soon?" It was still summertime, for chrissake.

"Soon? The primary is in September. I don't plan to lose this race."

Tubby told the judge he was with him all the way, and he had a smug expression on his face when he hung up the phone.

"Hey, guess what, Cherrylynn," he called out loud. "I'm going to be cochairman of the Judge Hughes Re-election Campaign!"

She ran in to hear the news. He did not immediately realize it, but his mental fog was starting to lift. She spotted it right away.

7

Charlie Autin was into martial arts, and he was usually never happier than when he was rearing back and kicking someone—laying a mountszu on them. Until he got involved with Daisy, and then she was the only thing on his mind.

He thought she must be older than she said she was, which was twenty-two, because she seemed so experienced about everything. The way she told it, she had only been on the streets a couple of nights before Charlie picked her up that first time. Even allowing for a certain understandable fibbing in that area, it was just amazing what she knew. Tarot cards, for instance. She could predict the future. He had tested her, like on the outcome of a Zephyrs baseball game—they would lose—and again on whether Charlie's boss would give him Saturday afternoon off—no—and she was right both times. She had traveled more than Charlie, and had even been to the casinos on the Gulf Coast. And sex was just crazy, it was so good. She could make Charlie crawl on the floor and beg for more.

Other girls he had dated lacked all of those abilities.

She agreed to come over and see his apartment on a side street near Bonnabel Avenue, in Metairie. It was in the back of a brick house with a little yard, and the owner lived up front. Daisy looked real hot when he picked her up, tight red slacks with some kind of gold fringe on them, and a low-cut white tank top that showed off a herd of brown freckles on her neck. They rode off into the deep canyon hidden in the lacy pink bra that peeked out around all the edges of her shirt. He had to sneak her up the driveway to his door in the back so old Mrs. Winters wouldn't have a heart attack.

"It's nice," she said, looking around the low-ceilinged living room furnished with a big TV, a glass-topped table, and his weight set.

He showed her the kitchen, which had a window looking out to the backyard, where Mrs. Winters was just now clipping the flowers off her ligustrum hedge. Charlie quickly closed the curtains. He let her see the bedroom next, which was filled almost wall-to-wall with his water bed. Charlie's idea had been to get Daisy into that immediately, but she backed away from the bed quickly and returned to the kitchen, bouncing her hips. He followed like a puppy dog.

"What you got to drink, Charlie?" she asked.

"Oh, beer, and Gatorade. I maybe got some Dr Pepper." He bent down and looked in the refrigerator.

"What kind of beer?"

"Some tall cans of Bud," he said, pulling one out of its plastic noose.

"I'll split that one with you." She sat down on the only chair in the room and crossed her legs.

"Sure," he said, popping the top. Daisy frowned when he started to hand her the can, and he got the message. She watched him trying to locate two glasses and shook her head.

"This place sure could use a woman's hand." It surprised her when she said that because it sounded like something her mother would have said.

"I do all right," Charlie said.

"Who does your cooking?"

"Popeye's." He laughed and poured her beer into a plastic Endymion cup. He gave up trying to find another for himself and leaned against the stove holding the can.

"Hrumph," she snorted. "You can't live on that."

"To tell you the truth, when I get off work I'm not hungry a lot of the time. It's all the fumes from the spray paint. I always want a couple of beers, but I usually ain't that hungry."

"You ever think that job might be bad for you?"

"Yeah, but it's what I know how to do. I'm sort of good at it, too," Charlie said proudly.

"How'd you learn how to paint cars in the first place?"

"My father and brother did it back home in Luling. I could have worked for them, but I got tired of living at home. You know."

"I know what you mean," Daisy said.

"Is that why you came to New Orleans, to get away from home?"

She studied her beer and her pink fingernails.

"Something like that, Charlie. I didn't really have no home. You ever heard that country song 'Fancy'? 'Here's your one chance, Fancy, don't let me down'?"

"Not really."

Daisy shrugged. "It's just a song. Let's say there wasn't much for me in Alabama, and they didn't line up to say good-bye when I caught the bus."

"I have a big family," Charlie said. "We get together sometimes and cook, man. They make lots of food— gumbo and shrimp, and they fry up lots of fish. Man, it's good."

"Maybe you ought to go back out to the country and live."

"No, there's no work. And a lot of people ain't too friendly to my family. I had a little trouble back home, too. My dad said it was time to get away and let it all cool down."

"What kind of trouble?" Daisy was interested.

"Nothing. I got caught with some dope. Nothing bad."

"You still mess with that?" Daisy asked. " 'Cause I don't."

Charlie, who had been about to pull open a drawer and offer her a joint he had rolled this afternoon, shook his head. "No way," he said emphatically.

"Good," she said, and smiled at him for the first time.

"You like living out there at the motel?" he asked.

"It's all right. I miss having a stove. . ."

"Well, you could come over here and cook, whenever you wanted to."

She laughed, and he thought her teeth looked very pretty, even though one was missing way in the back.

"I imagine you'd like having a cook around," Daisy said.

"Really, Daisy," he said. "You could come over here any time you wanted to. You wouldn't have to cook." Charlie blushed. Mrs. Winters would blow a fuse if she caught on, but he would think of something.

Daisy stood up and crossed the room to face him. She took his fingers in hers and looked up into his eyes.

"Don't get cozy with me, weirdo, unless you mean it," she said in a husky voice. "The only kind of man I want is one who can keep on caring."

Charlie swelled up with caring. He gripped her shoulders through the soft cotton top and pressed them tightly. "I ain't never felt this way about nobody before," he managed to get out.

"Just so you understand," she said, and gave him a hard squeeze below the belt.

"C'mon," she said, and led him out of the kitchen.

"It's good to be surrounded by such a brain trust." Judge Hughes leaned back in his pillowy leather armchair, hands clasped over his ample middle, and smiled affectionately at his guests. Tubby Dubonnet and the Reverend Horace Weems filled two of the large chairs in front of the judge's desk in his chambers at the Orleans Parish Civil District Court. Tubby had also just been introduced to a slender black man wearing a pinstriped gray suit, who now sat at attention in a smaller chair back in the corner underneath a lopsided ficus tree that touched the ceiling. His wire-rimmed spectacles were tinted a brilliant shade of orange.

"Mr. Dubonnet and Reverend Weems, as the co-chairmen of this mighty campaign into the future, you will, I am sure, carry this enterprise to its inevitable successful conclusion, guided and assisted by the all wise and knowing Deon Percy, who has agreed to serve as my campaign manager." He indicated the man under the ficus.

"Always glad to do my part, Alvin," coughed the Reverend Weems. He wiped his wide brow, the color and dimension of a hickory stump, with the spotless white handkerchief that he plucked from the breast pocket of his lavender suit of sturdy blended fabrics.

He had a mustache like a medium-sized paintbrush, and he rubbed it with his free hand while he turned to inspect Tubby. "This is the first time I have had the pleasure of meeting Mr. Dubonnet, but I am looking forward to sharing the task ahead with you, sir." He coughed again. "A touch of allergies," he added.

"It's going to be great working with you, Reverend," Tubby said. "What exactly do you envision us doing as cochairmen, Judge?"

"Why don't you answer that, Deon?" The judge pointed at the man with the orange glasses in the back of the room.

"We're going to be asking you to meet individually with major donors, and to give us names of people who might want to contribute. You will be invited to attend all the planning meetings, though attendance is not mandatory. You are respected pillars of the community, and your identification with this campaign has great value to us."

"Ah." Reverend Weems nodded.

"I don't know how well respected I am in the community," Tubby said. "I doubt I'll draw any big-time support."

"I'm sure that you're just being modest," Deon began, though in truth he had never actually heard of this particular lawyer before.

"People know you, Tubby," Judge Hughes interrupted. "More importantly, I know you. We got through Tulane Law School together. We took some hits, as you know, but we got through. I don't believe I would have gotten this job the first time I ran if you hadn't walked me through the halls of those big tall buildings downtown, shaking hands with all those old men on the letterheads who've never set foot in a courtroom and probably never thought about electing a black judge. I got in so good that, last time around, nobody ran against me. But things have changed," he said grimly. "I want you to do your old magic for me one more time."

"Okay, Judge, but I think most of the prominent lawyers already know who you are now, and by and large, they're going to support you."

Judge Hughes took off his bifocals and wiped them on his sleeve.

"I've got a theory about white people," he said. "They're forgetful. When I was growing up over by Carrollton, I couldn't buy me a soda in the drugstore. Back then the black voters, and there have always been a lot of them in this town, went with whatever white candidate laid out the most cash. I know that, and you probably do, too. That's the way it was until Dutch came along and we had our man in City Hall. When it was my turn to stand for office, I found that most of the whites who I needed also needed me. All of a sudden they were ready to forget the way it had been. Now, Tubby, I don't count you that way, of course."

Tubby raised his eyebrows, but didn't say anything.

"I got the white support I needed, and I've repaid that, I believe." The judge's voice was rising. "Now I need it again. But I don't want there to be any danger that my white supporters have forgotten about me. You've just got to remind them that Alvin Hughes is running for judge, and he's been a damn good judge, and by God I want some votes and some contributions when the chips are down." He slapped his palm on the desk and made Tubby, the reverend, and a paperweight jump.

"I see the direction you're headed here, Al," Tubby said. "Don't let them forget that good government isn't free."

The judge beamed and Reverend Weems nodded his weighty head.

"I'd say we ought to organize a committee of influential members of the Bar who support the reelection of Judge Hughes," Deon chimed in.

"We'll have to have several dinners, with tickets in several price ranges," the judge offered.

"And, of course, some parties in people's houses uptown and in the Garden District," Tubby said, stroking his chin.

"And a full-page ad, signed by lots of lawyers, in the *Times-Picayune*," Deon suggested.

"We will, of course, strive to see that our churches are also behind you," said Reverend Weems, not wanting to be left out.

"Right you are, Reverend," the judge agreed. "That will be critical. Because my opponent's father is Bishop Bloom, pastor of the Original Babylonian Missionary Pentecostal Church, and he'll pull a lot of ministers their way. But I don't want to overload you gentlemen with jobs right at the beginning. Deon's going to be drawing up a plan of campaign, and he will be communicating with both of you. And I've got to talk to the mayor and the councilmen and the other powers that be, and see how the deck is stacking up. And in five minutes I've got to get back on the bench."

Court was adjourned.

Judge Hughes escorted his shield bearers to the door of his office.

"I can't tell you how grateful and thankful I am for your willingness to help," he said as he shook each man's hand. He gave Tubby a wink.

Mrs. Evans smiled as they shuffled through the compact waiting room. The Reverend Weems was unfamiliar with these surroundings, and Tubby pushed him along gently until they were in the hallway outside.

A half-dozen citizens wearing JUROR badges lounged on the long pews facing the grand doors to the courtroom.

"I know we're not supposed to discuss the case, but that lawyer's perfume is making me sick," a plump woman told her companion.

"And you know that tall one with the mustache," her friend responded. "I don't think she's ever shined her shoes."

"I suppose this is where you do most of your work," the Reverend Weems wheezed as they walked toward the only working elevator.

"Hard to believe, isn't it?" Tubby laughed and pushed a button.

"I have no doubt that this is what God has planned for you," Weems said kindly.

Whom did I offend? Tubby wondered.

8

Daisy needed to go to work, but Charlie was stalling around, making conversation as they sat in his pickup, parked outside her room at the Tomcat. They had eaten dinner at the Picadilly Cafeteria and the evening was balmy, which was all nice, but now it was prime time to get to hit the sidewalk and pay the rent.

"How do you get the old guys, and you know, bikers to leave you alone?" Charlie wanted to know.

Daisy had told him that she never let herself be picked up by these two types of customers, which wasn't true, but Charlie kept asking her this kind of stuff.

"Charlie, I got to go," she insisted.

"How do you keep from getting hit on by the cops?" He was torturing himself.

A dark green Cadillac sedan pulled up and parked on her side. Its headlights switched off.

"Charlie, I told you it ain't pretty, but it's how I pay my bills. You got a better idea, you just let me know, okay?"

He frowned.

"Okay?" she repeated.

There was a tapping at the window, and Daisy jerked her head to see two strange men standing outside the truck. The one who had curly hair and looked like a bouncer at a strip show leered at her and tapped again. He was working his square jaw around a wad of bubble gum. The other guy looked like a dead coal miner.

"Open up, Daisy Chain. I want to talk to you," the big one said.

"Shit," Daisy spat and rolled the window down.

"Yeah?" The man looked familiar, like she might have done something with him a couple of weeks back. She was sure, however, that she had never seen the character standing behind Curly. He was thin like a stick with protruding ears and had hooded eyes that did not leave hers—very creepy.

"Tell john-john to get lost," the big guy said. "I got something private to say to you."

"Now wait a minute," Charlie said.

"Who the hell do you think you are?" Daisy demanded.

"I'm a representative of organized crime, Miss Daisy Chain. We don't allow independents working out here on the Airline. Now let's go discuss the situation." He reached inside the window and unlocked the door.

"Get out!" Daisy shouted angrily. She skittered over the seat next to Charlie.

Curly-hair grabbed her right arm above the elbow and yanked it hard.

Charlie grabbed her left arm and pulled it his way.

Daisy was swearing and Charlie was yelling at the man to leave his girlfriend the fuck alone.

They never saw the skinny man come around to the driver's side of the truck, but all of a sudden he pulled Charlie's door open.

Charlie tried to slap the man backhanded. He nicked the cheek a little before everyone saw the gun in his hand.

Charlie's lip curled up in an angry snarl over his teeth when the man stuck the barrel of his pistol between Charlie's eyes and pulled the trigger.

Pieces of skull splattered over Daisy, and the explosion deafened her. She stared in horror at the gunman's steady green eyes during the instant it took him to turn away and trot back to his car.

She saw the surprised look on the curly one's face. He let go of Daisy's arm and banged the door shut. Blinking, mouth open as if he might have something to say, he backed up to the green sedan. Then he got inside and the car lurched away from the curb. Its lights swept over Daisy's frozen face, and it rocketed off into the night.

Daisy was screaming, but she couldn't hear herself.

9

When it rains at night in New Orleans the streets seem to melt. The traffic lights make fluid stripes of red, yellow, and green that ooze on the shiny black asphalt like finger paints squirting out of a tube. They shimmer and dance to the beat of windshield wipers. Pedestrians huddle against the brick walls of buildings, clutching their packages, watching raindrops bounce over their shoes and gutters overflowing and bubbling along.

It was like that the night Dan died. Tubby drove down Magazine Street to the hospital, trying to remember to steer. He had gotten the call at home from one of the doctors, a man named Smaltz, he thought. All he could do when he replaced the phone on its cradle was to suck deep breaths and try to contain the pain.

Dan and he had known each other for a long time. Mixed-up memories of him collided like the rain drumming on the roof of the car. A much younger Dan, shooting cans of Miller in a college dorm, ripping a sink off the locker-room wall when he lost a wrestling match, arguing politics with anyone who would listen to him preach against the bourgeoisie, growing pot in the landlord's backyard—a forty-year-old Dan getting shot in the chest on St. Ann Street.

A tragic waste. The guy wouldn't hurt a fly, Tubby was thinking, squeezing the steering wheel so hard it hurt. Dan died trying to rescue me. He took my bullet.

That scene would always be vivid in Tubby's mind. Dan was lying spread-eagle on the street, a bubbly, bloody hole in the center of his chest. Tubby felt he was responsible, even though rationally he knew he really wasn't. It was Roux who had pulled the trigger.

Dan had been on the job, bellhopping at the Royal Montpelier, drinking immoderately and helping the rest of the staff mop up after the worst flood in modern history—the famous Mardi Gras deluge. Tubby had been caught by the flood, like everyone else. Exhausted and dazed, he had struggled to the Royal Montpelier where his old buddy had warmed him with whiskey, and found him a cozy bed in the room of a lonely tourist from Chicago. Things got complicated, and a bastard called Roux cut Dan down on the street, as easily as one might swat a mosquito.

But Dan had survived, after a fashion, in a hospital bed for five months. Until now.

• • •

There were a few hours, before he started drinking, during which Tubby adequately performed the role of attorney for the deceased. That is, he made arrangements for Bultman's to come for the body. He called Dan's aunt Melissa in Harvey and left a message on her machine.

"So sorry, Dan died tonight. You can call me."

With thirty-five cents he borrowed from a nurse, he called Detective Fox Lane at the Sixth District. She wasn't there either, but he left word that the Dan Haywood matter was now officially a homicide. As if that would make any difference. Fox, whom Tubby used to think of as a stellar officer, had dropped the ball when it came to ferreting out the person or organization behind the senseless murder. That investigation had dropped out of sight like a paper cup you kicked down a storm drain, like a dead woman sinking into a muddy flood.

Tubby fled the hospital, found his Chrysler, and let it carry him uptown. The rain had stopped, and the clock on the dashboard said 4:03 A.M. He parked outside Grits Bar, and he could see Janie, the barmaid, through the wire mesh that covered the smoky takeout window. She was pouring drinks for some pool players who wouldn't go home. It looked warm and comfortable there. Too comfortable for his angry thoughts. He drove on to the all-night K&B— for a bottle of Maker's Mark and a plastic go-cup he got for a quarter. Then he made his way to the river.

Sitting in the sand and straggly weeds, legs dangling over the bank, he drank his whiskey straight and watched dark oil tankers and grain barges moving slowly upstream toward Baton Rouge. Their rigging lights looked as delicate as fireflies. Across the wide black void of the Mississippi River, shipyards and power lines glowed like fairy castles.

Even for Tubby, sitting in the woods drinking straight whiskey while the dew soaked his jeans was bad form. He was too downhearted to care.

"You were a hell of a dude, Dan," Tubby yelled at the river and hoisted his cup. Tree toads croaked.

A scruffy mongrel, black hairs spiked in stiff clusters on his nobbly back and with a scrap of chain fastened to its scabby neck, circled the morose figure with his intoxicant, sniffing loudly and warily.

"C'mon in," Tubby yelled, spooking the animal back into the shadows and brush. Eventually, however, it came to sit quietly beside the lawyer, wild eyes intent on the shadowy vessels straining against the current. At some point Tubby reached over and gently unclipped the rusty chain. In time, his eyes closed. So did the dog's.

In his dream Tubby saw the faces of the dead. So many of them, he could not count. They stared at him through the portholes of a ship caught between the stars and the swirling black water. Some, like Dan, he knew, and tears squeezed from between his tight eyelids. Others, ghostlike, Oriental, dark-skinned, were strangers. Nearer and nearer they came, calling to him and singing words he could not understand. Arms, emaciated, reached out for him. He twisted and shook and cried out in his sleep.

A wet nose in his ear woke the lawyer up. His nighttime companion was hoping for food. A man in running shorts up on the distant levee was staring down at them. Tubby waved the dog away, and it loped through the wet grass toward the new candidate. Behind him the sun was coming up, and birds were chirping in the willow trees sprouting from the riverbank.

Tubby's jeans and shirt were wet where he had been lying on the ground. A lot of muscles he had forgotten about hurt when he tried to get to his feet. The white clouds spun around him, and he fell down again. An orange ladybug peeped at him over a blade of grass by his nose.

"Ah, me," he sighed. All well and good to be drunk at night in the woods, but in the daylight it would not be long before one of those well-meaning joggers with a cellular phone called 911.

With effort, Tubby got himself together. Trudging back to high ground he discovered, to his utter astonishment, that no one had messed with his car during the night. Sticking the correct key into the ignition, he could almost hear his daughter Collette saying to her sister, "I'm really worried about Daddy."

10

At the Daily Grind coffee house on Magazine Street, Collette Dubonnet spread lemon curd on her maple walnut scone.

"I'm really worried about Daddy," she confessed to her sister.

Christine blew the steam off her hazelnut latte.

"You mean because of his drinking?"

"Exactly."

"Daddy has always drunk a lot."

"I know, but now it's way too much."

"What makes you say that?"

"Have you talked to him lately?"

"No."

"Well, I called him at work, two days in a row, and

Cherrylynn said he wasn't there. Where is he, I asked, and she didn't know. So I asked if there was anything wrong, and you could tell from her voice that something was."

"What did she say?"

"Nothing, but you know how protective she is about her boss. It was the way she said it, though. I can tell she's worried."

"Hmmm." Christine was noncommittal.

"So I called him at home. One time I got his answering machine, and the other time he answered, but he was real gruff."

"You talked to him?"

"Yes, but his voice was kind of slurred. He said everything was fine, but he didn't sound right. I mean, he wasn't real conversational like he usually is."

"Hmmm." Christine picked at her croissant. "I know he's been feeling pretty bad about his friend Dan dying and all."

"Yeah, but he's got to get over it."

"I'm sure he will. And you know the older generation just drinks a lot more than we do anyway."

"It's so unhealthy."

"Look at Clarise's father. He won't even leave the house."

"Except to go sailing. And at their parties, all they do is drink like fish."

"And smoke. A lot of them smoke all day."

"They got that from their parents. All Grandad did was smoke and drink, smoke and drink."

"And parade at Carnival."

"I don't know how they survived."

"We're probably all brain-damaged from fetal alcohol syndrome."

"Really, it's a wonder we've got any brains left."

"And Mom, too, as long as we're talking about drinking."

"She'll go through a bottle of wine a day."

" 'Where's that damn corkscrew?' " Christine shrieked, mimicking her mother. Her sister laughed, and a law student at the next table, baseball cap backward on his head, lifted his nose from his *Black on Admiralty* to shoot them a curious glance.

"I'm worried about her just as much as I am about Daddy," Collette said.

"What do you think about Mom's boyfriend?" Christine asked.

"What? What boyfriend?"

The law student pretended not to listen.

You did not have to sit in the bushes by the Mississippi River to drink seriously in New Orleans. Tubby was proving that at the graceful bar called the True Course, a chic, dimly lit grill tucked away in the Warehouse District. Raisin Partlow, his running buddy for many years, had joined him. The good thing about Raisin was he was usually available, since he himself never worked. The women in his life did that for him. If they complained, Raisin never heard it.

Tubby's drink of the day was an Old-fashioned. Raisin was drinking Wild Turkey over ice.

"What's the song that guy's playing?" Raisin gestured at the piano player, white shirtsleeves tied high on his forearms, who was playing cabaret melodies for the scattered audience of men in jeans, sports coats and narrow ties and women in Moroccan-print blouses and skirts from Saks.

"That 'guy' is Harry Mayronne, Raisin. He's well known. He's playing the 'Surrey with the Fringe on Top.' "

"Watch the fringe and see how it flutters," Raisin muttered and lit a cigarette with a pack of matches from the bar.

"Rodgers and Hammerstein," Tubby added.

"I'm as corny as Kansas in August," Raisin said and tossed his match into the ashtray. He proudly exhaled a soft ribbon of gray smoke.

"Younger than springtime am I," Tubby replied and knocked back the rest of the red drink in its heavy glass. He signaled to the barman.

Raisin laughed and coughed.

"They cremated Dan," Tubby said. "I've got his ashes out in the trunk of my car."

"Jesus," Raisin said.

"I'm supposed to take some of them over to his aunt's across the river in Harvey."

"Is that where he was from?" Raisin asked.

"As much as anywhere, I guess. She raised him.

Dan's father was killed on an oil rig out in the Gulf when he was real little, and the mother ran off or something."

"He didn't get any money when his father died?"

"No, the way I heard it he got killed over a card game. It really wasn't work related. But getting nothing is probably what got Dan started in the union business."

"I remember meeting him just one time," Raisin said. "He was down here 'cause of some strike. Was it shrimp peelers?"

"Crawfish workers, I think," Tubby said.

"What the hell kind of union cares about crawfish workers?" Raisin asked and showed the bartender how much Wild Turkey he wanted transferred from the clear bottle to his glass.

"He always told me it was the Industrial Workers of the World, but I think he was pretty flexible about his affiliation."

"He could sure drink beer," Raisin said in admiration."I remember that much about him. And eat. I watched him put down two roast beef po-boys with extra gravy at Domilise's."

"Yeah," Tubby said and smiled.

"Where did you ever meet him?"

"He was my roommate during the year or so I was at McNeese State. We were both on the wrestling team, until we got kicked off."

Raisin thought that was funny. "How did Dan ever get way over in Lake Charles, Louisiana?"

"His high school coach got him a scholarship, just

like mine did. Neither one of us knew anybody in Lake Charles. We hit it off right away. He wasn't so much into politics then, but he was clearly crazy. He'd sniff shoe polish, eat shaving cream, race cars around the football field, steal the cheerleaders' pom-poms before the game, stuff like that."

"What a guy."

"Yeah."

They listened to the piano for a while.

"The last thing he said to me when I visited him a couple of weeks ago was 'I know him from the old neighborhood.' "

"He was talking about you?"

"I guess. He was looking at me." Tubby took a swallow and grimaced.

"You weren't really from his old neighborhood, though, were you?"

"Hell, no. I'm from north Louisiana, or whatever you call where Avoyelles Parish is."

"Maybe he was talking about Jesus," Raisin said, blowing smoke off into space.

"Or Joe Hill." Or maybe someone else, Tubby was thinking. He rubbed his jaw and drummed his fingers on the bar. Raisin watched him out of the corner of his eye.

"I'm gonna go make a phone call," Tubby said, and pushed off his brass stool.

The pay phone was in a wood-paneled alcove by the men's room. It smelled like lemon furniture polish. He dialed Flowers's number and, typical, got a recording that said, "This is the Fueres Detective Agency, please leave a message."

"Flowers, this is Tubby. I've got a job for you. Can you meet me in the office tomorrow at, say . . ." He was going to say one o'clock, his recent arrival target, but almost against his will he was getting that old fired-up feeling. ". . . at nine o'clock?" he concluded.

He hung up the phone and stared at a leaflet left in the booth advertising a riverboat with "Extreme Payoffs Every Night." All he could see in the dollar signs were dead men's eyes. And then his vision began to clear.

"I'm not from Dan's old neighborhood," he said to himself.

11

Tubby beat Cherrylynn to his office at the Place Palais the next morning. On her desk he found a pile of message slips from the Judge Hughes campaign, and more alarmingly, a fresh draft of Cherrylynn's resumé placed neatly beside her word processor.

He went to his private office, sat down at his desk like a man with a mission, and thumbed through a client's lease file his secretary had thoughtfully spread out for him while he waited for Flowers.

He heard the outer door open, but it was Cherrylynn's head that appeared.

"Mr. Dubonnet?" She was surprised.

"Good morning," he said solemnly, keeping his eyes glued to the file.

"You sure are up early today," she chirped.

"Have we any coffee?" he rejoindered.

"Why sure, boss. Give me a minute and I'll make a pot." She disappeared, happy to oblige his unusual request. Normally Mr. Dubonnet could flip his own switch.

"Bring me two sugars and a resumé," he muttered to himself.

He heard the front door open again, and a "Why, Flowers, I had no idea you were coming," from Cherrylynn.

She was bustling along behind the detective, unsuccessfully trying to show him the way to Tubby's office while fixing the stray red hairs on the back of her neck.

Flowers's tall frame filled Tubby's doorway. "Morning, Mr. Tubby," he said, showing off his pearly whites. Dark-haired, tan, lean, muscular, and well dressed, Flowers was good-looking by any standard. He was also sneaky and fast. Tubby liked having him around, though his presence unaccountably kept Cherrylynn in an agitated state.

"Can I offer you some coffee?" she asked as Tubby waved the detective forward.

"No, thanks, Cherrylynn. I've been drinking it all night." Reluctantly she left and softly closed the door behind her. Flowers settled himself in one of the leather armchairs and waited expectantly.

"I've got something I want you to check out," Tubby told him.

Flowers raised his eyebrows and nodded.

"You know my friend Dan Haywood died."

"I heard," Flowers said. "Sorry."

"Yeah, it's too bad. The guy who shot him was named Roux."

"How do you spell that?"

"I don't know for sure. When I heard it, I thought r . . . o . . . u . . . x, like you make gumbo with, but hell, it could be short for kangaroo for all I know."

"Okay."

"You probably know part of the story, since it was in the papers. I got mixed up with Roux when he took me and Marguerite Patino hostage after robbing a bank. It was during the flood, and Dan introduced me to the lady who gave me shelter from the storm. When I needed his help, he came looking for us, and Roux shot him. Then the police found a corpse that could be Roux, but it's so burned up it's hard to tell. Anyhow, the cops closed the case."

"Which makes them happy."

"Exactly. But before he died, Roux showed me a certain document he stole from the safe-deposit boxes at First Alluvial Bank that proved that Noel Parvelle down in Chalmette was getting screwed out of about five million dollars in an oil deal."

"This is getting complicated. Let me take some notes." Flowers fished a small pad and gold pen from the breast pocket of his jacket.

"It is complicated," Tubby said, "but I'm not asking you to understand the whole deal necessarily. I just want to find the people who were behind Roux. Or, on the off chance that it was somebody else's body that got burned up, I want you to find Roux himself."

"Okay, what can you tell me about him?" Flowers was starting to write.

"I can tell you he was shorter than I am and real thin. He dressed like he was from Texas—fancy boots, polyester jacket. He might be thirty-five years old. He's got big ears. And he's got these funny eyes."

"Funny how?"

"Scary, to me. They're hooded almost, like a lizard, and they're green, and when you try to look in them there's nothing there."

Flowers looked up for a second. "Good thing he's dead," he said.

"Yeah, if he is."

"Where would I start?"

"A couple of weeks ago, when I was visiting Dan, he suddenly says to me, 'I know him from the old neighborhood.' I was so blown away that he spoke that I didn't even think about what he was saying. But now, I think he might have been talking about Roux. Maybe he recognized the guy. That might explain why Roux was so quick to shoot Dan as soon as he saw him."

"What's the old neighborhood?"

"Dan was raised by his aunt in Harvey. Here's the address." Tubby slid a piece of paper across the desk.

"Okay, I'll talk to her, and then what?"

"And then, I don't know. Sniff around."

Flowers closed his notebook. He was frowning.

"I really want to nail the people who are behind all

this," Tubby said seriously. "They're big shots, and they're screwing up this town." He met Flowers's eyes. "Those were actually his last words to me."

" 'I know him from the old neighborhood'?"

"Right."

"Must mean something." Flowers stood up.

"Find out for me, please," Tubby said and watched the detective sweep out of the room with two long strides.

A moment later Cherrylynn appeared from the office's combination file room and kitchen with Tubby's mug of coffee. She was somewhat perplexed to find Flowers's chair empty.

"Missed him," Tubby said.

"He left already?" She looked around the office as if the detective might be concealed somewhere.

"Well," she said, recovering. She put the coffee carefully on the corner of the desk blotter. "Should I open a new file?"

"No, I've sent him out to find the men who killed Dan."

"Did you learn something new?"

Before he could try to explain it all, the telephone rang. Cherrylynn reached across Tubby's desk and grabbed it.

"Dubonnet and Associates," she shouted. "Oh, hello, Mr. Partlow." She checked Tubby for a sign. He nodded. "Yes, he's right here." She handed Tubby the receiver and discreetly slipped out of the room again.

"Hey, Raisin."

"I've got some bad news, pardner."

"What's that?" Tubby asked in alarm.

"I think Cesar was busted last night."

"Really? What for?" Cesar was an artist whose drawings of blues singers and street bums were semifamous. Tubby had known him since college, too. In fact, he was staring at one of Cesar's prints on the wall while he talked to Raisin. It was a drawing of people eating beignets in the Café du Monde.

"Cocaine, I think."

"Where did you hear this?"

"A friend of his called me."

"Where is he?"

"Central Lock-Up, most likely. He was arrested last night. He had a whole house full of people watching the Tyson–Holyfield fight."

That figured. Cesar was a good host and entertained a veritable salon of musicians, painters, oddballs, and losers, who liked to drink beer and watch sports all night on cable TV.

"How much did they catch him with?"

"Something like a kilo, is what I heard. It was supposedly a setup."

"Jesus Christ," Tubby said, aghast. "That's like a life sentence."

"Well, I wanted you to know. I'm sure he would have called you himself if he could."

"Yeah. Okay. I'm going down to the jail now and see if I can find him."

Tubby quickly got his jacket off the hanger behind the door.

He did not mess around when people he liked or who paid him well got locked up at Tulane and Broad. Jail in the Big Easy was a dangerous place.

He explained his mission to Cherrylynn and hustled to the elevator. The Hughes for Judge campaign would have to wait.

Templeman D was one of Sheriff Mulé's new concrete castles that stretched in a windowless, razor-wire-wrapped line for half a mile beside the Pontchartrain Expressway. Unless you drove a police car, no parking was permitted, and you got there by walking through four blocks of prisons and bondsmen—past police headquarters, Parish Prison, Traffic Court, Community Correctional Center, the House of Detention, and Central Lock-Up. The prisoners at Templeman were short-timers and pretrialers. They didn't get many visitors, anyway.

The fat black deputy wearing Sheriff Mulé's black uniform hardly looked up when Tubby pushed through the heavy glass door. She just held out her hand, palm up, for his ID. He kept his Bar card and his driver's license next to each other in a plastic case, just for such times.

"I'm trying to find Cesar Pitillero," he declared.

She consulted her computer and made a call. She told somebody to bring the prisoner in 4B down for a lawyer visit.

The trail led through a series of corridors and outdoor walkways, each stage punctuated by a rivet-studded steel barrier that had to be unlocked electronically by some invisible person deep in the nest. Finally you got to sit alone on a long row of blue plastic chairs until the prisoner was brought down. You met him in a booth with a pane of reinforced glass between you.

Tubby was allowed into the booth first, and he heard Cesar proceeding through clanging doors before a gaunt, black-bearded head appeared on the other side of the glass.

"Glad to see you, sir," Cesar said, cracking a wild grin that deepened the crevices in his face, making him look more like a Cuban boat refugee than he actually was. His outfit was color-coordinated—city-issue lavender sweatpants and a navy blue pullover with OPP stenciled in white letters on his chest.

Tubby asked how he was feeling.

"Everything's okay." The smile stayed.

"Well, what happened?"

Cesar stared at him dead-on. "A guy I barely know came to my door with a package and put it in my hand. Then all these policemen came in behind him and arrested me and everybody else in the house. We were watching the fights. They let the others go this morning. My bail is two hundred fifty thousand dollars."

"Man," Tubby exclaimed. "What's the charge?"

"Here's what they gave me." Cesar unfolded a packet of papers he had carried down from his cell. "Maybe you can figure it out." He selected a worn white sheet and pressed it against the glass for Tubby to read. His fingers were shaking.

"Distribution of a controlled substance. Cocaine," Tubby read. "Possession of marijuana. Three grams. Distribution?"

Cesar shrugged. "I was just watching the fights."

"Distribution is the worst they got. It could have been possession, or intent to distribute, but this is worse. How much cocaine was it?"

"A bag about this big." Cesar drew a picture about the size of a loaf of bread with his hands.

"That's a lot," Tubby said.

"Tell me about it." Cesar knew it was a lot.

"What about the three grams of pot?"

"They asked me where was my pot, and I showed it to them. They thought I was kidding. They were expecting pounds or bales or something. But that's all there was."

"Did they search the house?"

Cesar nodded.

"Did they find any money in the house?"

"They took about three thousand dollars from my bathrobe hanging on the bedpost. They said it was evidence."

"That's a lot of money to keep in your bathrobe."

Cesar nodded again. "I wasn't buying the cocaine. That's just where I keep my money. I was set up."

"Why?"

"If you can get me out of here maybe I can find out."

"Yeah, well that's a real stiff bail." Tubby was surprised it wasn't higher. Cesar's case had lousy facts. "Who set it?"

"I don't know his name. He was a white guy."

"Okay. I can find that out."

The lawyer tried to give his client an encouraging smile. Cesar smiled back. There was a tic in his cheek, and it didn't make him look so good.

"You got everything you need?" Tubby asked.

"I can't complain. I'm going to be here awhile, aren't I?"

"To be honest . . ." Tubby nodded. "What about the other inmates?"

"They're okay. I'm a star. Once they found out how much I was in for they think I must be a very super dude."

"Of course you are. Just ahead of your time. Or behind it, or something. I'll see what I can do."

"I'll be here." His eyes were like the dog you left behind at the pound.

Tubby walked out. He reclaimed his own ID and eventually stepped into the smoggy free air. He began his trek back through the jail kingdom in search of his car—thinking that an attorney is but one cog in a very frightening criminal justice machine.

12

Tubby believed that a lawyer must eat, and so he decided to take a chance that there would not be a long line at Uglisich's. It was only a few minutes' drive past the Clio (affectionately known as "CL 10") housing project. Tubby always told out-of-town visitors to the restaurant that the neighborhood looked worse than it really was. He braked hard to avoid butting a couple of kids who sped through a red light on their bicycles, yelling unintelligible warnings at each other and at him.

He approached the unpretentious eatery, crooked wooden siding painted gray, and entered its garlic-rich atmosphere. The small dining room was packed with a combination of guys with ties, white shirtsleeves rolled up, and a jazzier clientele wearing floral dresses, vividly colored T-shirts, sandals, and jeans. He was filled with an aching hurt for oysters or shrimp, but all the tables, and even the seats at the bar, were taken.

"Hey, Tubby." A familiar voice rose above the din.

Back in the corner Tubby spied the waving hand that belonged to Winnie Alphonse, a lawyer most noted for his mane of white hair and his pink Stetson cowboy hat.

"Come join me," Alphonse yelled, and Tubby squeezed his way through the dense thicket of chairs and shoulders hunched over bowls of gumbo and platters of crabs.

"Have a seat." Alphonse kicked the chair across from him, and Tubby fell into it gratefully.

"Man, it's crowded today," he said settling in.

"Timing is everything." Alphonse leaned back against the wall to permit a short, portly waiter to wedge in with a basket of French bread.

"Take your order?" the waiter asked Tubby between gasps.

"What are you having?" Tubby asked Alphonse.

"Red beans and rice. It's on my diet, except for all the sausage."

After scanning the blackboard quickly, lest his waiter escape, Tubby ordered shrimp scampi.

"Want some beer to drink with that?"

The prospect was appealing, but Tubby ordered a Barq's red drink instead.

He watched Alphonse attack his plate.

"So what's new?" his benefactor asked between bites. "I haven't see you around the courthouse lately."

"I've been trying to avoid stress."

"I had a law partner once," Alphonse told him. "Her idea of how to avoid stress was to go work out every afternoon at the New Orleans Athletic Club for about three hours. She'd jump rope and swim and do all those machines. Then she'd go to the steam room and get a massage."

"Yeah? How did it work?"

"It was tremendous for her. She liked it so well that she quit practicing law, and now she's got a TV show in Boulder, Colorado, where she teaches aerobic exercises." Alphonse mopped up his forbidden cheese and butter with a crust of bread and popped it into his mouth.

"I've been on a less drastic program," Tubby said, looking around the room. It wasn't much to see—stained walls, a couple of beer signs, and the kitchen right there where you could hear the pots banging around, but Mr. Uglisich could dish up the food.

"I just came from the jail," Tubby said.

"You got appointed to something?"

"No, an old acquaintance of mine got busted for cocaine."

"How'd it happen?"

Tubby told him the story.

"Sounds a little far-fetched—the part about being set up," Alphonse opined. "Do you think he's telling the truth?"

"Sure!" Guys who stayed up all night watching ESPN didn't do drugs, did they? "Of course there are a lot of details I don't know yet. The visiting area down there isn't really conducive to sharing confidences. Getting his bail reduced is going to be tough. There's no upside for a judge to make it any easier for a drug dealer to get out of jail, especially in an election year."

Alphonse patted his lips with his napkin. "Oh, there's always a way," he said. "Especially in an election year when the pressure is on to come up with money. A couple of thousand dollars to a person of influence might enable him to get out on a personal surety bond."

"You know such a person?" Tubby asked.

"It's possible that I do."

Tubby reflected upon that information. He watched the waiter storm out of the kitchen with what Tubby hoped was a large lunch for him. "Funny," he said. "I've been practicing for a long time, but I've never done anything like that."

"It don't always work out so smooth." Alphonse finished his bottle of Abita beer and wiped his lips.

"Shrimp scampi," the waiter announced, dropping a steaming platter in front of Tubby.

"Looks good," Alphonse said.

Tubby carefully speared a shrimp with his fork and studied it while it cooled.

"I don't think I'm ready to go that route," he said finally, and took the flavorful critter into his mouth.

"It's a bad practice," Alphonse agreed. "Your client, however, might take a different view."

Walking slowly to his car, under the weight of a substantial bowl of bread pudding and rum sauce for dessert, the good and the bad voices inside Tubby carried on an angry debate about where a lawyer's ethical duties lay in such a situation.

13

Sometimes, after the bar closed, the owner took a drink herself, up on the balcony overlooking the yacht harbor, with the stars twinkling overhead and the warm, almost salty air blowing over the lake for company. This was Monique's time by herself, while the bartender cleaned up downstairs and before she had to relieve her baby-sitter at home. She could think about life's little things. And about the big ones, like how she missed Darryl, her boyfriend, who had been killed beside the cash register below, and who had bequeathed her this hot spot known as Champ's.

Tired, Monique was holding a wet plastic cup full of cranberry juice and vodka and letting the breeze cool under her blouse. Sometimes it was hard to keep the ghosts out of her mind, and lately they were invading her sleep. Some of them were strangers. Suddenly she heard a long wail and saw a woman break from the shadows on the far side of the harbor inlet and hurl herself over the quay side into the black water.

"Jeez-o-flip," Monique exclaimed. "Jimmy!" she yelled, bending over the railing and waving at the window below. She saw the woman's arms flailing around in the water, agitating the yellow and blue reflection of the bar's neon lights.

"Jimmy!" Monique screamed. Getting no answer she pitched her drink over the side and ran back through the "chill-out" parlor used by important patrons, knocking over a chair in her haste, and clattered down the stairs.

"Call the Coast Guard!" she yelled. There was a patrol station right next door. Jimmy, stacking napkin holders by the light of a Bud sign over the bar, stared at her, befuddled. "A woman just jumped into the water!"

Monique pulled open the glass doors and ran onto the wooden deck where on sunny days sailboats docked and boys and girls greased each other with tanning oil.

"There she is. I can see her!" Monique pointed to midstream. A head, hair spread out in the gentle current, bobbed up and down.

"What's the number?" Jimmy was behind her.

"Goddamn it!" Monique cursed, plopping down onto the deck and pulling off her sneakers. "Jimmy

Fender, can you see that goddamn Coast Guard station over there? Run over there and get somebody!"

With that, Monique dove into the water and began splashing away. Jimmy pulled at his hair and set off running.

Trying to keep the engine-oil-flavored lake water out of her mouth, Monique flailed across the channel until she bumped into a limp, floating form. Trying to approximate a hold her Sunday school teacher had taught her long ago, she gripped the woman under the chin and clumsily began sidestroking back toward her tavern. It seemed to take a long time.

Men with flashlights were running onto the deck when Monique got near, and they reached in and dragged her and the floater out. One squatted down to perform CPR on Monique's catch. Another tried to do the same thing on Monique, who, operating on instinct, kneed him solidly in the groin. He rolled off her, howling.

With a gurgling sound, familiar at Champ's, the potential drowning victim vomited a large amount of Lake Pontchartrain and gasped for air.

Keeping his distance, the coastguardsman whom Monique had repulsed radioed for an EMT wagon, and before you knew it, the deck was swarming with guys in green coats. Five or six cops who had been patrolling the playground on the lakefront made their appearance, and for a while you could hardly move.

Everybody congratulated Monique and got an eyeful of her bod through her soaked clothes. One of the cops finally remembered his manners and got a blanket out of his car to drape over her shoulders.

The young woman Monique had pulled from the deep got strapped to a rolling stretcher. She was awake and crying. Monique stood over her and watched curiously. Their eyes met for a moment before the EMTs hustled their patient to the van.

Monique offered all the cops a beer, but they said no. One asked Monique for a date.

"I'd think twice about that, buddy," advised the coastguardsman whom Monique had popped. Finally they were gone.

"Man, that's a hard way to kill yourself," Jimmy said thoughtfully, smelling the lake water with distaste. "You didn't even think about it. You just jumped right in," he said, admiration showing.

"It ain't no big deal." Monique started to say "Anybody would have done it," but Jimmy was already shaking his head.

"I don't go into that water for nobody," he said. "It's full of gross shit I don't even want to imagine."

Monique shrugged. She knew there was worse stuff than dirty water.

"Tonight you close up," she said. "I'm going home for a shower."

Jimmy let her out the front door. Monique still had the blanket wrapped around her. Normally she took a bicycle to and from work. Her apartment was only about four blocks away.

"You gonna walk?" Jimmy asked her as she set off down the street.

Monique just waved good-bye. She felt great, as if her life had a purpose. Like a nun in her brown habit, Monique shuffled along the deserted pavement.

The cop who had asked her for a date flashed his lights at her, and she let him give her a lift.

Flowers pulled to the curb in front of a small white house badly in need of paint in a neighborhood of welding shops and plumbing contractors. He walked to the iron-barred security door, rang the bell, and waited.

Presently, a timid voice within asked who he was.

"Sanré Fueres, ma'am. I'm the detective who works for Mr. Dubonnet. We spoke on the phone."

Aunt Melissa Haywood, a white-haired wisp of a woman in a pink quilted housecoat, opened the inside door tentatively.

"Could I see some identification, please?" she asked.

"Sure." Flowers got out his wallet and handed her through the bars a plastic card with his picture on it.

She inspected him and the photograph carefully. "I guess this is you," she said and used a key to unlock the security door. "Can't be too careful nowadays."

She led the way into a living room crowded with a lifetime of furniture and pictures. She offered him a Coca-Cola.

"Thanks. I'd like one very much," he said, and sat on a yellow vinyl-covered chair while she slipped away to the kitchen. Flowers jumped up and quickly sniffed around the room. He glanced over the calendars and photographs on the walls and the electric bills laid out on a small desk. It was a habit with him. He was settled quietly on his chair by the time she returned with a glass of Coke and a paper napkin.

"There. Now how can I help you?" She sat down softly by the desk.

"Mr. Dubonnet has a theory that the man who killed your nephew might be somebody Dan knew, someone 'from the old neighborhood.' "

"I'm afraid I don't know who any of Dan's friends are. He hasn't lived here for, oh, twenty years or more. He was a good boy in some ways, in that he called me up on my birthday. He sometimes seemed to know when I needed cheering up, and he'd just call. But he hardly ever visited." She frowned. "Since his father died, Dan never seemed to like it much around here. His mother ran off when he was born, I guess you know."

"No, I didn't. Maybe the killer was somebody Dan knew as a kid, Mrs. Haywood. Somebody named Roux?"

"No, I don't think so," she said, concentrating. "I do have some of his high school albums, if you think that might help."

"Sure." This was the exciting part of detective work. The tiny woman made her way to the back of the house and soon came back with three dusty yearbooks from Harvey High, home of the Harlequins.

She placed them on Flowers's lap and opened the purple one on top to a page with the corner bent over.

"That's Dan," she said, pointing a crooked finger to a large, fierce-looking face, surrounded by a mane of black hair, straining against a tie and a collar that were too tight for his bulging neck. A little tear fell on the page.

"He was a handsome boy," Flowers said.

Mrs. Haywood backed away and sat again in her chair. Flowers kept his eyes down and started flipping pages.

There was no one with the name of "Roux," so he started at the beginning of the alphabet. A clock on the wall whirred.

Suddenly a name jumped off the page. Willard LaRue. There they were, the big protruding ears. The LaRue boy had a crew cut. There was a cockeyed smile on his lips, but his eyes told a different story. They said, "Get out of my face."

"Do you know this boy?" Flowers leaned over to hand the book to Mrs. Haywood.

"That's Tex. Yes, I know him. He was always into trouble. We called him Tex because he wore a Roy Rogers hat, but I remember now his last name was LaRue. That poor boy was in a pickup truck one day and it rolled over his daddy and killed him. Can you imagine? They lived in a house on Almonaster Street. I remember it had a big tree in the front yard that they tied Dan to one time—just being boys, I guess. I don't know what happened to Tex and his mother. Her name was Mamie."

Flowers nodded. He stood up and stacked the albums on the desk behind Mrs. Haywood.

"Thanks a lot for the Coke," he said. "I'm real sorry about your boy. Can you tell me where Almonaster Street is?"

"I'm going there right now," Flowers told Tubby on his cellular phone. "I knew you'd want to hear about it right away."

"Willard LaRue," Tubby repeated. He was sitting in his office downtown. "Where are you now?"

"I'm turning onto Almonaster Street as we speak. We're right by the Harvey Canal. Half the houses are boarded up. And here's one with a really big tree in the front yard. I'll call you when . . . now wait a minute."

Flowers watched as a slight man wearing a cowboy hat emerged from 6039 Almonaster Street and turned to lock the door.

"Tubby, I think Mr. 'Roux' is coming out the door right now. I'm passing the house and pulling over. We'll see what he does."

"Follow him!" Tubby's voice broke up in static, it was so loud.

"You got that right," Flowers said softly and clicked the phone off.

He parked in front of a bread truck, beside an open ditch sprouting orange flags where some sewer repair project had been halted, maybe for lunch—maybe for the year. LaRue got into a sea-blue Ford Taurus that could have been a rental, and crunched away from the curb. He passed Flowers without a sideways glance and turned right at the next corner. Slowly, Flowers set off in pursuit.

In tandem, they got onto the West Bank Expressway and immediately got off at Manhattan Boulevard. Flowers followed his quarry past a series of gutted shopping centers and low-rise apartment complexes and saw LaRue hit his blinker once and enter the parking lot of a one-story, windowless institution.

The detective drove past. The sign out front said SWEET MADONNA MANOR.

Looking at his mother was like looking at a trapped rabbit, LaRue always thought. Same frightened, dumb expression. Even before she had started to lose it and gone to the home, he had thought of her like that. His old lady had never been someone to inspire confidence.

Visiting her was no picnic, that's for sure. He didn't know why he did it. Except she had been good to him— as good as anybody could be with a psycho like Le-Rocca LaRue for a husband.

Looking at ol' Mom in her bed always brought it back—the endless afternoons spent practicing how to tie a lariat, how to lasso a fence post, how to be a quick draw with a chrome six-shooter. In Harvey, Louisiana, for chrissakes. Just some fantasy his old man had. But he couldn't let it alone.

He'd beat the shit out of Willard at the drop of a hat. And beat the shit out of Mom if she got in the way. He probably wasn't too happy when Willie popped the pickup into reverse and flattened the asshole like a pancake on the cement driveway, but with his skull cracked he wasn't in any condition to complain.

Despite himself, LaRue chuckled. His mother, wig askew and all gums, just looked at him like he was the wolf who had come to dinner.

"You don't have a clue, Mom," he told her. Fact was, she didn't.

14

The Hughes Campaign was rolling, and the phone in Tubby's office was beeping nonstop.

"We appreciate your support. Al certainly won't forget it. Lemme give your name to his campaign manager," were becoming his main lines.

Joey Pureloin, the assessor in the Seventeenth Ward, called to get the word out that he was also up for reelection and expected to be on the mayor's ticket. He wanted to assure Al Hughes of his "unquantified support."

Sam Aruba, who said he was a constable in Marrero, asked what he could do. "Tell your New Orleans friends to vote for Al," Tubby suggested.

"I got lots of 'em. You know Bernie Fawn?" Tubby did not.

"Really? Oh, well. We've got a fund-raiser out here at the American Legion Hall," Aruba continued. "The judge can come if he wants to."

"Thanks, but what's the point? That's not in his district."

"It's a blast, man. Free beer and chili. Where else you gonna get on the TV news for kissing a nutria? It's free exposure."

"Makes sense to me. I'll give your name to Al's campaign manager. And thank you for your support."

A spokesperson for Louisianians Opposed to Offenders Now called to invite Judge Hughes to a forum on crime.

"Yeah, but you know he's a civil court judge. He doesn't sentence people to jail," Tubby explained.

"Then I should report to our committee that Judge Hughes refuses to come?" the spokesperson asked indignantly.

"Not at all." Tubby backpedaled swiftly. "Let me give your name and number to his campaign manager."

"I think you're going to have to screen my calls," he told Cherrylynn, but a minute later she beeped him to say that Judge Carlo Trapani was on the line.

"I see on this letter I just got that you are chairman of the Hughes reelection campaign," Trapani announced in his trademark voice, loud as a fish peddler's.

"Cochairman, actually," Tubby said.

"Anyway, I'm calling you because I want the judge's support in my election. I am prepared to give him mine.

Under the table, of course, since we judges aren't allowed to endorse candidates. Stupid rule, huh?"

"Yeah," Tubby said.

"Even though I'm on the criminal bench I think incumbent judges should stick together for the good of the profession."

"I'm sure Al will be happy to hear that, Judge. Have you tried to talk to him directly?"

"I've called Al twice and left messages." Judge Trapani's tone was sour. "He has not yet returned my calls."

"I know he has been very busy," Tubby began. Hell, he was thinking, now I'm Al's damn secretary.

"So am I," Trapani yelled.

"Yes, well I will certainly see that he gets your message."

And he would, because he had learned that one of the matters of Judge Trapani's docket was the prosecution of Tubby's friend Cesar Pitillero, for the distribution of cocaine.

On a lighter note, Adrian Duplessis, beloved by the populace of New Orleans as Monster Mudbug, called with a most unexpected bit of news.

Tubby took the call with trepidation because the Monster generally was calling from jail where he frequently landed for municipal offenses like parading without a permit. By trade a humble tow-truck driver, Adrian's claim to fame was riding the streets of the city dressed as a giant, boiled crawfish, surrounded by mermaids, in his rolling cookpot known as the Monster Mobile.

"I ain't in jail, Mr. Tubby," were his first words.
"You'll never guess what."

"Marcia Ball is going to ride on your float at the
Mandeville Seafood festival."

"Not quite that good." The Monster laughed. "She
only does that for the Moss Man." The Moss Man was
Adrian's idol. "But I'm working on it. I just qualified to
run for sheriff."

"What?" Tubby exclaimed.

"Yeah. I just got back from City Hall. I paid my
money and everything. I'm running for sheriff."

Tubby closed his eyes and asked him why.

"Just for publicity. You know, to get on television.
And I learned that, if I don't win, I get to keep all the
money people give me."

"Who would give you money, Adrian?"

"Nobody, probably, but don't you think it's a terrific
stunt?"

"I don't know about that." The sitting sheriff, Frank
Mulé, was one of the most powerful politicians in the city,
had about a thousand deputies on his payroll, and was not
known to have the slightest touch of any sense of humor.

"My slogan is 'A Crawfish Pot in Every Cell.' "
There was a click on the line. "Excuse me," Adrian said,
and the lawyer was about to slam down the phone when
Adrian came back on. "I gotta go, Mr. Tubby. Channel
Six is on my other line, and they want to interview me."

Tubby got up and strolled to his outer office to impart
this little vignette to Cherrylynn. She thought it was a
great idea.

"They need to do something to liven up these elections. With Monster Mudbug in it, at least we'll get some good parades."

The phone on her desk buzzed, and she answered it, looked surprised, and pushed the hold button.

"Sheriff Frank Mulé wants to talk to Mr. Tubby Dubonnet," she said.

Tubby's smile disappeared. He went back to his office. Closing the door behind him, he sat down and cleared his throat. Then he picked up the phone.

"Hello, Sheriff."

"Counselor, I see you're in politics now."

"Just helping out where I can."

"Good, 'cause Al Hughes is going to need all the help he can get if he wants to be reelected. I'm tilting his way, but I need to know if he's going to line up behind me. Is he for me or against me?"

"Are you expecting any opposition?" Tubby asked, being cagey.

"No. I just found out that that nutcake Monster Mudbug has qualified, but he's just a joke. I don't think anyone else is stupid enough to run against me. But I'm not sitting on my hands. I want one hundred percent support from every elected official in the parish."

"I'll sure let the judge know that."

"I'm calling you because every time I see your name there's some kind of a fuckup."

"What's that supposed to mean, Sheriff?"

"You know you've been messing with me. You defended that drug pusher Darryl Alvarez. You dropped that habeas corpus on me that time I got some drug-dealing asshole locked up in Mississippi. I keep score. I know you've been a pain in my butt. I'm calling you now to be sure everything is lined up. I got nothing against Al Hughes. But if him, or any of his people, are gonna fuck with me, I'm gonna push back hard, no crap."

"Cool down, Sheriff," Tubby said. "I don't have a problem with you. I'll give the judge your message."

"You do that," Sheriff Mulé said, and hung up.

He's a whacko, Tubby said to himself, and he took a deep breath to try to calm down. A scary whacko.

Daisy didn't remember the part where they pumped out her stomach. She woke up, drowsy from drugs, in a room without windows, and it took her a couple of days to convince the shrinks and the social worker that she could walk down a public sidewalk without jumping in front of the first truck that passed. The cops were under-standing. The same ones who had come to the parking lot when Charlie Autin had been shot came to visit her in the hospital. Both were big guys, and they acted like they felt guilty, maybe, for just letting her go home af-ter they took her statement and she cleaned the blood off her face, the night of Charlie's death. She could have used a social worker then.

Daisy could remember drifting along the streets and crying. If she had encountered somebody selling crack on the corner, she would have copped it in a minute, wiping out a year of getting straight. That's how sick she felt. But all she found was cheap whiskey.

She had no explanation for how she got way out to the lake, but she remembered jumping in. The sensation, when the warm water closed over her head, was of ultimate pain relief. They told her that a woman named Monique Alvarez pulled her out. Now that Daisy was starting to get her mind sorted out again, she planned to make her amends.

After a long bus ride from Canal Street, she got off on Robert E. Lee and asked directions to Champ's Bar. The air-conditioning, when she pushed open the door, felt harsh to her. It was midafternoon, and the place was not crowded. A hippie bartender pointed out a slender brunette sitting at a table in the corner by a window full of sunlight, bending over a notebook.

Daisy walked up and cleared her throat.

Monique started. "Yes?" she inquired.

"Are you the one who pulled me out of the water?"

Monique's eyes rounded. "I sure am, honey. Won't you sit down?"

"Okay," Daisy said, pulling out a chair. "I came by to apologize for causing you so much trouble."

"Oh, no," Monique said. She reached out to pat Daisy's hand, but her visitor jerked it back. "That's such a strange thing to say. It wasn't any trouble, really. I'm just glad I was there to see you when you jumped in. You did jump, didn't you?"

Daisy nodded. "I wasn't in my right mind exactly. You see, my boyfriend got killed that day."

"How horrible," Monique said slowly. "Can you talk about it?"

"I don't want to burden you with my troubles."

"Honey, your accent is getting to me. Where are you from?"

"Loxley, Alabama, if that means anything to you."

"This is totally odd," Monique said. "I'm from Brewton. Did you go to high school in Epps?"

"Sure."

"What year did you graduate?"

The two women covered that territory, finally coming up with the name of a guy they both vaguely knew, and Monique got Jimmy to bring them both glasses of Perrier and lemon.

"I was glad to get the hell out of Alabama," Monique said, playing with the water droplets on the table's smooth surface.

"With me, it was more of a case of had-to-go," Daisy said.

"Have you been in New Orleans long?"

"Just a couple of months. I was thinking about moving on when I met Charlie." She sniffled.

"So what happened?"

"Two men shot him in front of my motel, right in the head. I was sitting right beside him in his truck. He didn't do nothing. He was just standing up for me."

Monique started shaking, though so quietly it was hard to notice.

"That's horrible. I know what you must be feeling."

"How could you?" Daisy demanded angrily.

"My fiancé was killed right behind you at that bar," Monique said. "His name was Darryl Alvarez. I was upstairs when it happened."

"Damn. Did you see who did it?"

"Yes. I think I know who it was. One of them got killed in the French Quarter. The other one is probably still around. It takes a long time to get over it."

"Have you?"

"I still think about Darryl. I didn't know him that long, but he was good to me. He left me this bar."

"I didn't know Charlie but two weeks." Daisy began to sob softly. "And he didn't have nothin' to leave."

"There, there." Monique patted her shoulder.

Later, after they had talked some more, Monique told Daisy that there was a lawyer named Tubby Dubonnet who might help her. He had helped Monique get her affairs straightened out. Perhaps he could kick the police in the butt until they brought Charlie's killers to justice.

"I ain't interested in no lawyer," Daisy said.

"He's actually more like a friend."

Daisy shook her head.

"I got my own plans," she said. "Lying in that hospital bed, I had a chance to think. What I came up with is I'm gonna get the son of a bitch that pulled the trigger myself. That's what made me get up and get out."

"Just how are you going to do that?"

"I don't exactly know yet, but I will."

Monique told her if she needed any help, just pick up the phone.

15

"I lost him. That's all there is to it," Flowers told Tubby. His face registered his discomfort. "He passed a truck, and for a split second I couldn't see him. So I passed the truck, and he wasn't there. Obviously, he turned right when I was out of sight. Juvenile mistake on my part." Flowers was troubled. "Fucking *diablo*," he muttered.

"What?" Tubby asked.

Flowers shook his head.

"It could happen to anybody," the lawyer consoled him.

"I guess," Flowers replied. "I've got my man, Jackson, watching LaRue's house, which turns out to be his mother's house. There's a nurse at the old folks' home who promised to beep me if LaRue shows up there again."

"Just let me know when you find him."

"What will we be doing then?" Flowers, always curious, inquired.

"I'm going to try to arrange a meeting with him and talk him into leading me to his boss."

"How?"

"I don't know yet." Tubby leaned back in his leather chair and stared at the painting behind Flowers's head. "I'll have to think up something that appeals to his nature."

"Might be better to break his legs first."

"That's a possibility. LaRue trusts me just a little bit, though, from the last time we met. When he kidnapped me, I led him to believe I might be somewhat crooked. A lot of the loot from his bank robbery was never recovered. LaRue may think I ended up with it. If I did, he'd be really impressed with me."

"But you actually didn't."

Tubby smiled and shook his head. A lady tourist named Marguerite Patino had managed to get out of town with a sack of Krugerrands, diamonds, and Rolex watches that LaRue and his men had stolen from the safe-deposit vault at First Alluvial Bank. More power to her.

"It's not my business, Tubby, but why don't you just turn LaRue over to the police?"

"How am I gonna turn him in? You don't even know where he is. But even if you did, most of the witnesses against him are dead or way out of state. I'm sure he has a convincing alibi, and the people he works for are powerful enough to manipulate the police and the court system." Truth was, the police were tired of hearing Tubby's theories about a crime czar.

"That's a hypothesis?" Flowers asked.

"That's my working assumption," Tubby said firmly. "There's some sick, dangerous mind, some menacing force, at the core of our city. That's what I want to root out, Flowers."

"Whew." The detective gently lowered his pen. He wasn't positive, but he thought Tubby was serious. "That's a very tall order. Usually I just bust people for cheating on their wives."

Tubby studied Flowers's face to see if he was being cute, but all he got back was that wide-eyed, innocent stare.

"Yeah, well you got to do something with your life," the lawyer said. "You can't just steal widows' pensions and get criminals off all the time."

"So we're going to do good?"

"What's wrong with that?" Tubby tried not to smile. "There may be a way to make some money out of it."

"You're the boss. If you want to clean up the city, sounds like kicks to me."

"The first step is to find LaRue. Again."

"I'll find him. He has stung my professional pride."

"God help him, then."

Flowers got up, and Tubby followed him out. He had a Judge Hughes campaign meeting to go to—another investment in good government.

He would cash it in one day.

16

The Al Hughes campaign was excited to locate its cochairman. A meeting of the entire brain trust was scheduled for that very afternoon in the Fellowship Hall of Reverend Weems's St. Pious the Third church. Although frazzled by his emergence from the alcohol-based cocoon in which he had dwelled for the past month, Tubby promised to be there.

The aging brick edifice of the St. Pious the Third church rose high above the slate roofs of the shotgun houses on Orleans Avenue. Many of the residences needed paint. A stray dog investigated the dented trash cans on the sidewalk. But the church itself glowed with respectable prosperity.

New black asphalt covered the parking lot, the lines

freshly painted yellow. The first half-dozen spaces were reserved, according to neatly printed signs stuck in the flowery border, for the pastor, the associate pastor, the music director, the chairman of the deacon board, the church secretary, and the custodian. The lot was half full, and Tubby saw Deon trotting up the concrete steps to a solid metal door, open at the side of the building. He followed and entered the long pea-green hallway festooned with children's drawings, in time to see the campaign manager huddle with Reverend Weems beneath the framed portrait of a brown-skinned Jesus. He could not hear what they were saying, but his "Good morning, gentlemen," caused the Reverend Weems to jump.

"Mr. Dubonnet, so good to see you, so good to see you," the reverend said warmly and clasped the lawyer's hand in both of his own. He pumped heartily. "Go right into our meeting room. Have some coffee, and we'll be under way shortly."

Judge Hughes, three men whom Tubby did not know, and Kathy Jeansonne, a newspaper reporter, were standing around a silver urn swapping jokes and grinning like crocodiles. He went to join them.

There were hellos and introductions all around, and Tubby shook hands with Lewis Pardee of the political action group COMP, Amadee Nesterverne from DINERO, and Johnny Papaya "from the mayor's office."

"And I know this lady. How are you, Kathy?"

"Fine, Tubby." The tall redhead eyed him suspiciously. Tubby did not usually call her a lady. "I look forward to working with you," she managed.

"What?" he asked in surprise. "Aren't you still with the *Times-Picayune*?" Jeansonne had on occasion reported unfavorably on Tubby's clients, and he had, in the spirit of revenge, fed her irresistible tidbits of misinformation.

"I took a leave of absence to work as press liaison on the campaign," she explained.

"Reporters can do that?" he asked, but her answer was cut off when Reverend Weems and the campaign manager joined the party. Judge Hughes suggested that everyone find a chair and get down to business.

"Ahem," the judge began from his place at the head of the table. "Deon, why don't you take us away."

"Greetings, everybody," Deon told the room, his eyes fixed on a pile of notes. "Since our last meeting, which most of you were able to attend"—he shot a significant glance at Tubby—"we have made steady progress. We have identified those sectors of the community where we must target our greatest efforts, and we have begun to build our war chest. Brother Pardee, maybe you and Brother Nesterverne can report on the efforts to secure the endorsements of your respective political organizations."

Brother Pardee, a gentleman in his thirties with a well-cut, three-piece black needle-striped suit of admirable thread, gold rings and wristwatch, and a face as smooth and brown as a chestnut, looked troubled when he said that no firm decision had yet been made by COMP (Communities Organized for Maximum Progress). In fact, he expected a tough fight from certain forces within the organization who supported the judge's opponent, Benny Bloom.

"What's it going to take for the COMP endorsement?" Deon wanted to know.

"I'd say about six thousand dollars."

Tubby woke up.

"The regular contribution is five thousand dollars for city races," Pardee continued, "but where there's some opposition within the organization I estimate that an extra thousand dollars will be needed to smooth the wrinkles away."

"I guess we all knew this race wouldn't be cheap," Deon said. "Okay, Brother Nesterverne, how are your people looking?"

"Our executive board met last night," said the slight gray man with a wispy goatee, whose hands waved constantly in the air while he spoke, soothing ruffled feathers. "I was able to bring the vote around to Judge Hughes—unanimously, I might add."

There was polite applause around the table. DINERO (Dollars Invested in New Orleans Region Only), as everyone knew, was one of the largest grassroots organizations in the parish—fully capable of flooding the streets with campaign workers on election day who would wave signs at motorists, stuff leaflets into mailboxes and under windshield wipers, and drive old ladies and drunkards too weak to walk to the polls.

"What's the cost?" Deon asked.

"The organization is requesting a contribution of ten thousand dollars," Nesterverne said solemnly.

Tubby whistled, and everybody looked at him.

"That's a lot of money for one poor judge to raise," Hughes said woefully. "I could see that much if I were running for district attorney or sheriff, but not for judge."

"The expected contribution for the sheriff's race is twenty thousand dollars," Nesterverne said, sticking to his guns, sculpting feather pillows with his hands.

"What do you say?" The judge looked at Deon.

"Eighty-five hundred would be more like it," his campaign manager said sourly.

"Amadee." The mayor's representative spoke up for the first time. "You guys are getting too expensive. See if DINERO won't come onboard, and I mean full stroke, for eighty-five hundred. If not, get your chairman to call me, and we'll see what can be worked out with my discretionary fund."

"Glad we're all on the same team," Tubby said. "How much do I get?" There were a few chuckles around the table, but not from the mayor's man.

"Your job is the giving, not the getting," Deon said. "Here's a list of all the members of the Bar the judge wants to tap for support. Most were with him the last time around. You can add as many more names as you can think of. All will be contacted by mail, and some by phone, to solicit their endorsements and plan receptions, etcetera."

"I could put on a crawfish boil in my yard," Tubby suggested.

"Swell idea," Deon responded.

"We'd have lots of beer, and corn on the cob, and boiled potatoes and mushrooms. I could grill some smoked sausage and maybe even some oysters."

"I believe I'll attend that party," the Reverend Weems boomed.

"I project a media budget of two hundred seventy-five thousand dollars," Kathy Jeansonne broke in, deflating the conversation.

"Holy smokes!" Judge Hughes exclaimed. He rocked back so far in his chair that he nearly tipped over.

"Want to break that down for me, Kathy?" Deon interjected.

"Sure. I recommend emphasis in three areas. First is yard signs. Five thousand signs at three dollars apiece is fifteen thousand dollars. Second is black radio. A ten-second spot and a thirty-second spot played with increasing frequency on gospel, soultrain, and rap programs on the five radio stations that target the African-American audience equals thirty-five thousand dollars. Third is television. A thirty-second 'positive' ad, which we begin three weeks before the election, and a thirty-second 'response' ad to smear dirt on our opponent, in response to whatever attack he makes on us, which we will blanket the airwaves with during the final four days. Cost—two hundred and twenty-five thousand dollars."

"Damn, 'scuse my French, pastor, but I'm not running for governor."

"With all due respect, Judge, the last governor's race cost the major candidates over four million dollars. What I'm projecting is the minimum amount needed to win at the parish level. You can bet Benny Bloom is seeing these same figures. And look at it this way, it's only about five dollars for each vote you'll need to get elected."

"You might get better results just handing out five-dollar bills," Tubby suggested.

"You can't hardly get 'em for five dollars anymore, Mr. Dubonnet," the mayor's man said sadly.

"And that's not legal," Kathy fumed.

"Of course," Tubby said quickly, "I was just kidding."

The gentlemen from COMP and DINERO were both studying the ceiling.

"What makes you think Benny Bloom is going to be attacking me, anyway?" Judge Hughes asked, a doleful expression on his round face.

"Because you're the incumbent, and that's how it's done," Jeansonne said in a tone sometimes used to send five-year-olds to the corner. "And in this case his media consultant is Bridges and Madison. They're famous for attack ads."

"Yeah, you're right," the mayoral representative said. "They worked for us in the last election. They're nasty guys."

"Better be prepared then," Deon said. "Part of Miss Jeansonne's job is research, and she has already begun digging up the, let's say, unpleasant facts about Mr. Bloom's career."

"Yes, according to his ex-wife . . ."

"Please," said Judge Hughes. "I'd rather discuss this somewhere else."

"Right," said Jeansonne and snapped her notebook shut.

"Thank you," Deon said. "We may have to tweak that media budget somewhat and see if we can trim some fat. But it gives us all a target to work toward. Mr. Papaya, can you give us any kind words from the mayor?"

"The judge has the mayor's blessings, and he will be on the mayor's ticket. Barring unforeseen circumstances, our people will be out there in force on election day, pushing the ticket."

"What unforeseen circumstances?" Tubby asked.

"If I knew, they wouldn't be unforeseen," Papaya said.

Good answer, Tubby thought.

Judge Hughes let out a belly laugh. "No comeback for that one," he said. "Does that about wrap it up? I've got a banquet to go to."

"I believe we've got it," Deon said. "Reverend Weems, will you give us the benediction?"

17

Daisy began her search for the nameless killer with the hooded eyes by connecting up with the mob. It was easy. An acquaintance of hers from the Tomcat Inn, who was in the same line of work, knew the telephone number of a guy named Courtney, whom she described as a white pimp. He collected cash from the girls as a licensing fee for being permitted to stand out on Airline Highway with their dresses hoisted up to their panty lines. Daisy went to the pay phone outside of the Taco Bell and tried the number. She got voice mail.

"Hello. My name is Daisy. I'm trying to reach Courtney. I want to start work tonight. Call me at this number right away." She recited the number on the pay phone.

She was halfway through her Tostado Supreme, sitting on the grass, when the phone rang.

"This is Daisy," she said to the smoke-scented handset.

"Do I know you?" It was a man's voice, husky.

"Yeah. I'm the Daisy stays at the Tomcat Inn. Where do I sign up?"

"You the Daisy that was there a week or so ago? There was an incident."

She almost choked. "Yes. That's me," she whispered. She knew the voice now. It belonged to the man with the curly hair who had put the arm on her, who had acted surprised when his partner blew Charlie away.

"What are you up to, lady?"

"I ain't up to nothing. I need to work, don't I? You don't want to talk to me, fine, but don't give me no more trouble, either."

"I'll talk to you. Be at your room at nine o'clock."

"I'll be outside my room. We can talk in the fresh air."

"Okay, but don't pull no shit."

"Same to you," she said and hung up.

Daisy was sitting on the curb outside Room 119 at the Tomcat Inn, swatting mosquitoes, when Courtney drove up in his Cadillac Seville. She felt herself starting to flip out when she saw the car, but she pinched her thighs hard to stay in control. Courtney was alone, and he sat by himself in the big car for a minute, looking around.

Apparently satisfied, he climbed out and sniffed the

air. He was a big man with broad shoulders, and his tan blazer threatened to pop a seam. He had on jeans and penny loafers, and a heavy gold bracelet on his wrist.

Daisy did not get up when he sauntered over, just watched him steadily and blew cigarette smoke in the air.

"Hey, Daisy," he said, thumbs in his belt. He took off his sunglasses to polish them on the sleeve of his jacket, and she saw that his eyes were like crowder peas with woolly caterpillars crawling over them.

"Hello," she replied, and snuffed her cigarette out in a crack in the concrete.

"You wanna talk inside?" he asked.

"No. Here."

He breathed loudly, but then sat down beside her, his knees at a level with her nose.

"You called me," he pointed out.

"Your name is Courtney?"

He shrugged.

"Never mind. I need to go back to work, and I don't want any more trouble."

"If you want to stay out of trouble," Courtney explained, "you've got to be part of the organization. The whole city is that way now. You can't be a independent anymore, not around here."

"Okay, so what do I have to do?"

"Somebody will come by every day at a time I tell you and collect a hundred dollars. You've got to pay it. If you want to do extra work, like a private party, you can call me on a phone number I'll give you, and I'll tell you what the deal is. If somebody places a special order and you fit the bill, or if we need an extra girl, we'll call you. In that case, you drop what you're doing, or who you're doing, and get ready. The pay is good for special jobs. If you want to get on the A list, you have to get tested for AIDS. You can go down to the blood bank and try to give blood. They'll test you. Some like a girl to be clean. Some don't give a shit."

"What if I don't have a hundred dollars a day?"

Courtney put his glasses back on.

"Then you get off the street and don't come back. It would be better for you to leave town."

She nodded and watched the trucks roar past on Airline Highway.

"About the other time," Courtney said. "Things got out of hand."

Daisy couldn't speak. A tear formed in her eye.

"Anyway, you won't be seeing that guy again."

"Why?" she asked sharply. "Has he gone somewhere?" Finding the guy who had pulled the trigger on Charlie was the whole point.

"No, he's around. He's just doing other things."

"Okay." She was relieved.

"Now, let's go in your room and have a little toot and, uh, consummate our understanding."

"Fuck off," she said, standing up. "I've got to go to work." She walked off toward the highway. She just wanted to be away from him.

Courtney laughed at her back.

"See you tomorrow," he yelled after her.

18

An important meeting was taking place in the office of the Empress of Saigon Restaurant. The most influential men were present. Hung Phat, thin and dapper in sharply creased slacks, mustache like a sudden charcoal stroke above his lip; Nuong Cuoc, burly with sleeves rolled up tight over his oysterman's biceps, and an eight-inch wisp of black hair growing out of his left sideburn; and Rolling Sam, the youngest of the group, barely in his twenties, who favored silk suits, sported a Rolex, and wore a fedora indoors. All were guests of the chairman of the board, in fact if not in name: Binh Minh, or "Bin Minny" as he was generally known.

Their host, whose restaurant this was, had provided

cups of tea and something stronger, a glass of Scotch, to Rolling Sam.

Pleasantries had been exchanged in their native tongue but, in deference to Rolling Sam, who by virtue of his age and public school education was limited in that regard, the substantive meeting was progressing in English.

Nuong Cuoc was holding forth, eyes darting around the room.

"We can be sure no one from our community is responsible. No one here would shoot three men to death on the side of the road and shoot up Mr. Singh's karaoke bar, not without me finding out who it was."

"So violent," Hung Phat observed.

"I beat up three, maybe four boys, but they didn't know anything," Nuong said.

"How about Mr. Singh?" Rolling Sam asked. "What does he think?"

"He doesn't know who did it. He's overcome with grief. His son is dead. His girls, Binh Ho and Oyster Lady, ran away, so he can't make much money. The police cleaned him out when they took over the bar. He expects us to see that justice is done. He is having visions of drifting souls who cannot find rest. He has laid this matter in our hands."

"When we locate the men in that car, they will be killed in a way that will be remembered," Hung Phat said quietly. "Then his visions will stop. The problem is to know where to strike."

Bin Minny, who had not spoken until then, laid down his teacup.

"I think I know why the girls ran away," he said. The others waited respectfully. "I think there is an effort now beginning to consolidate all of the businesses under one general. I think that our days of being left alone to manage the affairs of our community are coming to an end. There are many signs of this. Those who supply my product have reported to me that they have been approached and threatened by some people who do not want them to sell to me. It would not surprise me if those boys who got killed, Xuan and the others, had not been likewise warned to get out of the prostitution business. They would have laughed at that, of course."

"Anybody who gets in our way gets his nose cut off," Rolling Sam volunteered.

"Yes, that's right," Bin Minny said affectionately. The young man reminded him of himself at that age, when he had been a lowly corporal in the Army of the Republic of Vietnam. Similar aptitudes for intrigue, loyalty, and violence had enabled Bin Minny to rise to the rank of colonel before the fall.

"Whose nose we gonna cut?" Hung Phat demanded.

"I have an idea about that, too," Bin Minny said, "but there are still some doubts. I will need to talk to some people myself. Perhaps in a few days we can meet again and make a correct plan."

The others nodded.

"Why don't you eat now? My kitchen is yours."

In a melodious language, punctuated by laughter, the assemblage discussed their meal and the issues of the world. Rolling Sam sipped his Scotch and grinned when it seemed appropriate.

No child should go nameless, but Tubby had to swallow his fist when he learned that Debbie was going to name her youngster Arnaldo after Marcos's father. Seems there was some traditional imperative in the father's family that required this honor. As a sop to the Dubonnet line, for a middle name the poor child got stuck with Bertrand, after Tubby's father, whom everybody had called "Bat."

"Arnaldo Bat?" he repeated in dismay.

"No, Dad. Arnaldo Bertrand. We'll probably just call him Arnie."

"Arnie?"

"What's wrong with Arnie?" Debbie's voice was rising.

"No, nothing, nothing at all. There are lots of great Arnies."

"I know," she agreed. "But I liked Cody, myself, and Ashton and Forrest. There was this family tradition thing, though."

"I'll call him Arnaldo," Tubby said.

"I knew you'd like it. He looks just like you."

Artfully mollified, Tubby forced himself to concentrate on the enchanted swamp of parish politics. At home the night before, he had seen Benny Bloom's "attack ad." It had begun with a picture of a black man in handcuffs being pushed into a police car. Then a gavel came down, and the word GUILTY flashed on the screen. Then the docket of a court record appeared briefly before a hand, wielding a top-secret stamp, obliterated the page. The announcer said, "The file Judge Al Hughes doesn't want you to see. In 1974, Alvin Hughes was arrested for DWI. He was found guilty and required to pay a fine. This is what Al Hughes doesn't want you to know. Now you know the truth." An American flag filled the screen, and a new voice proclaimed, "And that is why those who know support Benny Bloom for judge!" Unmistakably, the speaker was Judge Carlo Trapani.

Tubby couldn't believe it. Half the people in town would know that voice. Trapani was supposed to be lined up behind Al Hughes.

Even more depressing, the next ad had shown Sheriff Frank Mulé throwing beads from a Mardi Gras float, and he was actually laughing. The sheriff was even more frightening when he stepped out of character.

All day long Tubby had been barraged by press packets faxed from Kathy Jeansonne, the campaign's media liaison, announcing at what church bazaar Al Hughes would be spinning the roulette wheel, at which school fair he was judging the crawfish race, at what gymnasium he was coaching "midnight basketball."

The judge had been seen kissing babies in Storyville, make that babes, the press release quipped.

Who's writing this stuff? Tubby wondered. He noted that his own name, correctly spelled, appeared on the letterhead of each press release. It took real mental effort to keep from thinking about the legacy he was leaving Arnaldo "Bat," Jr. Candidate Hughes had been endorsed by the Lesbian and Gay Political Action Committee, as well as by All Ministers Combined, which Tubby was enlightened to learn was an organization, in the words of one local pundit, of politically savvy evangelical zealots formed to combat the twin evils of video poker and free condoms.

The lawyer was exceedingly grateful when the phone rang and it was Flowers.

He had found LaRue.

19

They drove across the bridge together, then through a tangle of old neighborhoods and car dealers, to a bar on a side street in Harvey. The word was that there was a room in the back of the tavern where LaRue holed up. Cool air, smelling of old smoke and fresh beer, greeted them when they pushed through the doors. A noisy crowd was at the bar. A few couples were scattered at tables in dark recesses.

"Look, there's Tubby Dubonnet! He's running the Judge Hughes campaign," announced a stocky man at the center of the loud crowd, and Constable Sam Aruba stepped up to pump the lawyer's hand. Tubby was quickly swallowed up and introduced to the bartender and a bunch of other guys and told to get anything he wanted.

"This is my turf, buddy," Aruba yelled, "and we're gonna treat you right," he said, slapping Tubby on the back.

Flowers drifted off to exchange words with a fat black dude sitting by himself and drinking beer. At a table in the corner behind them, a muscular man with curly hair and a small woman in a tight skirt smoked cigarettes and looked around.

"Lemme see about something," Aruba whispered loudly into Tubby's ear, and he went back to the corner where the lady was sitting. She stood up and followed him back to the bar.

"Lemme introduce you to a sweetheart," Sam said, pushing the skimpily clad female at Tubby. "Her name is Daisy." Wink. Wink.

"Uh, pleased to meet you. My name is Tubby Dubonnet."

"You don't have to be on no formal basis," Aruba yelled merrily.

Daisy's eyes widened.

"I think we know somebody in common," she said in a low voice. "Monique, I think her name is."

"At Champ's Bar? Sure. What's your name again?"

Daisy already regretted telling Tubby about Monique, and she was about to make up a name when Flowers shoved his way into the pack and whispered into Tubby's ear.

"LaRue's in an office in the back. Right past the men's room."

"Gotta use the can," Tubby explained to the girl, and he left her and Constable Aruba standing there.

With Flowers in the rear, they walked into a dark corridor where doors marked KNIGHTS and QUEENS faced each other. Farther down the hall was a door with a crooked red sticker pasted on it that said PRIVATE. Flowers put his ear up to it and listened. Then, bracing himself against the wall he raised his knee and crashed his foot into the wood right above the knob.

The door banged open, and, as the detective and Tubby barged into the room, the man who had been napping on the cot inside sat up. His hideaway was furnished with the bare essentials, a small refrigerator, the cot on which LaRue had been sleeping, and about twenty cases of beer stacked along the walls.

Flowers's right hand was inside his coat, where he kept his gun.

Tubby had his hands out. "Peace," he said.

"What the fuck?" LaRue said, eyes darting around.

"We met at Mardi Gras," Tubby said. "Remember me?"

LaRue certainly did. "No," he said.

"I'm here to talk," the lawyer explained, stepping forward. "Let's all be calm. I want to talk business."

Flowers moved to Tubby's left where he could keep an eye on both men.

The doorway filled up with the big man who had been sitting out front with Daisy.

"Need help, partner?" he asked, checking out the splintered door frame.

"Maybe," LaRue said, adjusting his shirt collar and running a hand through his black hair. "Stick around, Courtney."

"Why don't we all come in and have ourselves a meeting," Flowers suggested.

Courtney obliged and stepped in, creating an opening for the lady who had crept up behind him.

Daisy had a tiny .22 pistol in her hand and popped off the first shot as soon as she glimpsed a slice of LaRue's head.

"No!" Tubby yelled and slapped at the gun.

She was firing again when Flowers pushed Tubby out of the way with such force that he smashed into the boxes of beer.

Courtney grabbed at the gun with his left hand and at the same time loosed a meaty right hook that connected with the whole side of Daisy's head. Reflexively, before passing out, she pulled the trigger again and shot a hole through Courtney's palm.

"Goddamn!" he shouted, bending over in pain and clutching his gushing hand between his knees. Daisy was out on the floor. LaRue and Tubby, both unhurt, locked eyes.

"Get her out of here," Tubby told Flowers out of the side of his mouth. He gestured to the woman spread-eagle unconscious on the dirty tiles.

The detective stepped around Courtney and scooped up Daisy. He loaded her onto his shoulder. Her little skirt rolled over her fanny, revealing purple silk with a frayed rip.

"I'll be right behind you," Tubby promised.

Flowers disappeared, and Tubby backed slowly toward the door.

"You saw me knock the gun away," he told LaRue. "I probably saved your life. I've got business to discuss with you that's worth a lot of money. You know my name. Call me, so I don't have to come looking for you again."

LaRue didn't budge from the bed, but his dead eyes were following Tubby as the lawyer faded into the hallway.

Tubby moved smartly. The sound of gunfire had emptied the bar. No Constable Aruba, no guys drinking beer, nobody. Flowers, the girl still slung over his shoulder, was silhouetted in the entrance, waiting for him. As Tubby trotted outside he saw the bartender's bald forehead poke timidly above the scarred mahogany.

Daisy got tossed into the backseat of Flowers's black Honda, and they blew gravel spinning out of the parking lot.

20

Daisy revived while they were speeding over the Crescent City Connection, the barges on the Mississippi River far below. Her eyes teared up while she fingered her jaw, and she did not speak.

Flowers dropped them at Tubby's car, as his boss directed. He wasn't paid to question his employer.

Tubby asked Daisy if she could walk. She nodded, and he told her to get into the Chrysler. She went without protest or comment.

"What's the plan?" Flowers asked.

"I don't know. Call me in the morning."

Tubby didn't speak again until he had his Le Baron started up and rolling toward Lee Circle. He kept one

eye on Daisy, seated beside him, lest she produce another weapon.

"What did you shoot at LaRue for?" he asked finally.

"That's his name? To kill him, what do you think?"

"What for?"

"Why did you stop me?" she asked instead.

"Partly just a reflex. Partly because I have other
plans for him." Tubby couldn't help noticing the curves
of her legs and thighs pressing against the upholstery,
so he didn't try.

"Monique at Champ's Bar told me you were a lawyer
and that I ought to talk to you. What were you doing in
that place with that man?"

"It's a long story."

"So's mine."

"Where do you want to go to tell it to me?"

"I have a motel room, but I think it's time to move."

"Then I'm going to take you to my house."

"Oh, yeah?" She tried to arch an eyebrow on the
swollen side of her face and winced.

He turned the car toward the river on Nashville
Avenue.

"Yeah," he said, almost to himself.

Walking across the dark yard, Tubby saw that his living room light was on. He did not remember leaving it
that way.

He motioned for Daisy to stand behind him while he
worked the key in the lock. Pushing the door slowly
open, he cautiously stuck his head inside.

On the couch, staring at him, was his daughter Christine. She was spooning yogurt from a plastic cup and talking on the telephone. The TV was on, but she had switched off the sound so she could concentrate on her conversation.

The sight of Tubby's escort stopped her in midsentence. With her lips open in a sort-of smile, Christine continued to nod her head as if listening to the voice of the phone, but her mind was elsewhere.

Daisy stood still, just inside the doorway, inspecting the room. A purple bruise was spreading around her left eye.

"That's my daughter," Tubby explained. "She has a key and shows up when she's least expected. Why don't you sit down, and I'll get you something to drink."

Christine pressed a button and put the phone down.

"Hi, Dad," she said.

"Daisy, this is Christine. Christie, this is Daisy." He smiled at them.

Christine stood up politely, then they both sat down on the sofa.

"Daisy is, uh," Tubby began. "Well, why don't you explain while I put on a pot of coffee?"

Daisy pulled her blue sequined chop top down to cover more of her rib cage.

"A country girl from Alabama," she said tensely. "And I should be getting out of here."

"Nonsense," Tubby said. "You need to clean up your face, and I need a drink."

The phone beeped. Christine dug it out of the

crack in the cushions and handed it to her father with scolding eyes.

"It's probably for you," she said prettily.

He took it and headed for the bar.

"Hello?" he said, spooning ice.

"It's me." The voice belonged to Marguerite Patino, and his mind raced back to a hotel room in the French Quarter they had shared for one special rainy night.

"Hi, Marguerite," he said slowly, his ice cube dripping on the rug. He had neither seen nor heard from the woman since she had departed on the day Dan got shot. She had been on his mind though.

"Am I interrupting anything? Is someone there?" she asked.

"Well, no, not exactly."

Dead silence.

"My dog is with me," Tubby said, recovering quickly.

"I didn't know you had a dog."

"He's visiting. Listen . . ."

Tubby woke up with the sunrise and tried to figure out how he had ended up all alone in his house.

The first one to go had been Christine. She had made an early departure after failing to elicit much information from Daisy.

"You look a little tired, Daddy. You ought to get some rest," had been her parting shot.

He had gotten Marguerite off the phone right away. She had sounded more than a little angry about the brush-off, and had not called back even though she said she would.

Then over coffee and a couple of shots of bourbon, Daisy had told her story to Tubby.

"So, what do you plan to do now?" he asked.

"Same as before. Kill LaRue." She shrugged.

Tubby explained his theory that there was a central crime boss over LaRue and Courtney and all the crooks. He would prefer it if Daisy waited until he had entrapped that person before she offed anybody. Daisy, however, made no promises. Tubby suggested that, perhaps, in some way she could help bring the "big guy" to justice. Daisy said she would like that, but she had a program of her own. Stay in touch, she told him.

And then she was gone, too. Tubby urged her to stay the night. She could have the spare room, but she was already out the door.

"Where can I reach you?" he asked the miniskirted figure crossing his yard. She apparently had no qualms about prancing around like that in his fairly sedate neighborhood.

"I'll have to let you know," she replied and kept moving until she was lost in the shadows of the oak trees that shrouded the broken sidewalk.

So he woke up alone. It was shortly after the sun came up, when he padded barefoot downstairs to pour himself a good morning grapefruit juice, that he discovered he was not alone after all.

"Sheez," or something like it involuntarily escaped Tubby's mouth when he walked into the kitchen and found Willie LaRue, cowboy hat on his head, sitting at the round table at the window, like a scene from a Greyhound station. LaRue was calmly building a stack of wooden matches.

"You're a late sleeper," LaRue said. He demolished his miniature log cabin with a careless tap of his pinkie finger.

"If I'd expected you to visit I would have gotten up lots earlier," Tubby said, trying to get his breathing back under control and his bathrobe cord tied. Any residual sleepiness had fled.

"I thought I might catch that whore here," LaRue said. He sounded disappointed.

"No, I'm here by myself."

"I know. I already checked."

Tubby went to the cupboard and found a mug. He got his pitcher of cold-drip coffee out of the refrigerator.

"How did you get in?" he asked.

"Backdoor." It was disconcerting that, while LaRue's hands stayed on the table and his body did not move, his head rotated to track Tubby around the room.

The home owner was depressed to see that a pane of glass had been busted out of the door. The shards were in the backyard.

"I guess I should complain to my alarm company," he said.

"It's not exactly a state-of-the-art system," LaRue remarked.

Tubby poured his coffee over ice and sat down at the table to face LaRue.

"So what do you want?"

"You tell me. You said you wanted to talk."

"Not to you. To your boss. Whoever put together the bank robbery, which I know was just a cover-up to steal a counter-letter from one Noel Parvelle's safe-deposit box. The purpose of your whole robbery was to get that one document to set up an oil deal. I've got a deal of my own, and I need a partner. I think your boss is a likely candidate."

"Then let's go. He's waiting for us right now."

So, twenty minutes later, Tubby was riding in LaRue's blue Ford Taurus up Carrollton Avenue. LaRue drove with the same exterior calm and interior intensity he conveyed when he conversed, or when he attacked, as though the reactive part of his brain functioned on a precise automatic pilot.

"No blindfold?" Tubby asked, trying to get a rise.

No luck. LaRue's response was a tic of his cheek that might have been one ingredient in a smile. It was just as well because Tubby needed the time to figure out what he was going to say to LaRue's boss. That part of his plan had not yet gelled in his mind. He had been too busy fantasizing about finding the guy. When they cruised past the College Inn, where in more relaxed moments Tubby had enjoyed many a sloppy Ruben sandwich, he still had no clue about what he would say. It began to dawn on the lawyer that he might be in some danger.

"Where are we going?" he asked when they passed under the interstate.

"You're going to get some breakfast." This normally inviting sentence sounded menacing coming from a man whose pointy jaw didn't seem to move when he talked.

Tubby pursed his lips. He looked out the window at the familiar restaurants they were passing—Angelo Brocato's, Lemon Grass, Jamaican, Venezia—and tried to think. How had he imagined this part when he explained things to Flowers?

Without bothering to signal, LaRue hooked a right into the parking lot of Shoney's in Mid-City. He put the Taurus between the yellow lines and cut the engine.

"Are you kidding me?" Tubby demanded.

"Time to eat," LaRue replied, stepping in to the sun.

"I've never eaten here in my life," Tubby protested, climbing out with less gracefulness than LaRue had shown.

"Good morning. Smoking or nonsmoking?" their perky waitress chirped. Tubby wrinkled his nose trying to identify the odor wafting in the chilled air. Hash browns? Lots of them.

"We're meeting the man sitting in the booth over there." LaRue brushed past her. Tubby smiled and followed.

On a plush red upholstered seat, framed by a picture

window with a view of the palm trees in the parking lot, was Sheriff Frank Mulé.

He was by himself, hand on a cup of coffee, smoking a plug of a cigar, watching their approach.

"Oh, Mr. Mulé," the hostess said enthusiastically, since everybody knew the sheriff. She trailed her new customers closely, carrying a pair of menus the size of checkerboards.

"Howdy, Sheriff," Tubby said. He slid into the booth across from the portly elected official. LaRue snuggled in next to Tubby.

"Do you know how our buffet works?" the hostess asked.

"Not now, dear," Mulé said, waving his cigar at her.

"I'd like to hear about it," Tubby said, being difficult.

"It's all you can eat for five seventy-five. And the selection is really neat. Or you can order from the menu."

"The buffet is what I'll have," Tubby said. "What are you guys having?"

"Just coffee," Mulé said. LaRue nodded, looking absently out the window, meaning that coffee was all he wanted, too.

"Well, then you just help yourself," the hostess said, "and I'll get your coffee."

"Be sure it's all on one check," Tubby told her. "I'm paying for everybody."

She left smiling.

"Because this is my party," Tubby concluded.

"So, my man here tells me you've got something to say."

"Yeah, and why am I not surprised I'm saying it to you?"

Sheriff Mulé shrugged. "So talk," he said.

"You know, for a long time I've been trying to figure out who could have enough clout to pull off the big jobs in this town and never get caught, or even investigated. Now I know."

"Now you think you know," Mulé said, venting smoke. "Actually you don't know shit."

"Don't get me wrong, Sheriff. I'm not putting you down. I'm saying this with admiration. Of course it has been you. When there's drug smuggling out in Terrebonne Parish and somehow a boatload of drugs gets away, you are there. When the old mob boss Joe Caponata gets whacked, it's the night he's going to have dinner with you. When the safe-deposit boxes at Alluvial Bank are ripped off to camouflage the theft of one piece of paper, and so-called local investors turn that piece of paper into millions of dollars, why sure, you're a local investor."

"Why are you dragging this out?" Mulé asked. "I'm very busy." He squashed his cigar on a saucer.

"I'm just figuring a lot of things out. But it doesn't matter. Here's the deal. Is it okay if he hears?" Tubby pointed at LaRue.

"Rue, go over there and have a seat."

Whether LaRue liked it or not, he didn't show. He slid out of the booth and moved to a table nearby, out of earshot, but from which he had a clear view of the back of Tubby's head.

"Okay, Sheriff. Have you ever watched women's boxing?"

"I've seen 'em bite and scratch each other at the jail, if that's what you mean."

"No, no, I'm talking about the ring. Prizefighting. Just like men."

"I've heard about it."

"Well, if you've never actually seen it, it's an exciting sport. And it's not just tits and ass, like you might think. It's an organized sport. They've got an association and everything. The association ranks the boxers, decides who the champion is, stuff like that."

Mulé shrugged.

Happy Holly returned with coffee, reminded Tubby that he could "belly up" to the buffet, and learned that everything was fine.

Tubby leaned over conspiratorially and got closer to Mulé. A plan had formed in his mind.

"Women's boxing is going to be big. Very big. I've got an exclusive option to buy a franchise for Louisiana, Texas, and Mississippi. Let me explain. The cost of a franchise is reasonable, but it's more than I can handle alone. And I need certain things arranged. Here's what I have." Tubby stuck out his hand and began ticking off his fingers.

"I have the league's option. I have the boxers. I manage the premier female fighter in Louisiana. Ever hear of Denise DiMaggio? No? Well, she's hot. She's all the time over at Coconut Casino in Mississippi. I've got a line on the perfect place to erect the arena. I'm talking first-class. Down by the river near Napoleon Avenue. And I've got half a million bucks."

Mulé smiled, the way an alley cat does when it's got a rat's tail in its paws. Tubby winked at him.

"And here's what I ain't got, Frank. I ain't got the other half a million I need to close the deal with the league and get up and running. And I ain't got the site for the arena locked up. I could probably get the money somewhere else, though I figure for you, with all the stuff you're into, it should be a piece of cake. The tougher thing is getting the property. It's not exactly available, and it needs to become available. Seeing how you planned the bank job, and seeing who you got working for you . . ."—Tubby looked over his shoulder at LaRue—"I thought I'd come to you first."

"Where's the property you're talking about?" Mulé wanted to know.

"You may be familiar with it. It's right beside the Napoleon Avenue wharf. A company known as Export Products used to lease part of it. So did a company named Bayou Disposal. Then the Casino Mall Grande people decided it would be a great location for a gambling boat to dock. They've got the lease on it now. I know, because I sold the lease to them, representing Export Products. Now I want it back."

"How do you propose to get it back?"

"Here's where my intuition comes in, Sheriff." Tubby took a sip of coffee. I should have been onstage, he thought. "I speculate that you and the casino crowd are in the same mud hole, so to speak, that you play in the same dirt, that if you tell them you want the fucking lease, they'll give it to you. They may want a piece of the action in exchange, but hell, riverboat casinos aren't worth what they used to be, so they'll make a deal. And if they won't, you'll run them out of town."

"You've got a big mouth, Dubonnet." Mulé's face had turned a couple of shades redder.

"You're damn right, Frank. I project that as soon as the first bell rings, the arena is going to gross two hundred fifty thousand dollars per fight. That's the gate plus the television. On top of that, you can bet the fights over the telephone to Las Vegas. And I manage the fighters, get what I mean?"

Mulé's beady eyes were studying Tubby. His hairy fingers beat a tattoo on the Formica.

"It's a cash cow, is what I'm telling you." Tubby summed it up. "A damn erupting volcano of cash."

Mulé stared at him in silence.

Abruptly he pushed his heavy behind out of the booth and stood up.

"I'll think about it," he said.

LaRue was on his feet.

"Tell you what," Tubby said quickly. "Come see the girls. I can fix up a match especially for you. We'll make it real private. If you see it, I know you'll like it. We can talk business some more after."

Mulé stroked his chin.

"When and where?" he growled.

"Make it Friday night," Tubby suggested. "Say, ten o'clock. You know where Swan's Gym is, under the bridge?"

Mulé nodded. LaRue watched in silence. His eyes said he'd like to mash Tubby's face.

"The night's on me." Tubby winked.

The sheriff pointed a stubby finger at Tubby's nose. "I'll be there. If I do decide to do a deal, I'll want to see your cash. I'll want to see that right away."

Tubby opened his mouth to say more, but Mulé was threading his bulky body through the tables and was out the door. Tubby watched the two men cross the parking lot and pause to talk beside LaRue's car. Then the sheriff went to a black Cadillac, got in, and drove away. LaRue backed out and followed him.

Tubby got stuck with the check and had to spring for a cab to get home. On top of that, he didn't have a half a million dollars.

21

The first person Tubby told was Judge Hughes.

"Thing is, Al, I don't believe you want to get too close to Sheriff Mulé right now. I'm going to try to take him down, and I think he's going to fall hard."

They were having eggplant parmigiana and amberjack at Katie's.

The judge patted his lips with his napkin and studied his iced tea.

"That's an incredible story," he said finally. "Tubby, I share your strong feelings about what must be done with the sheriff, of course. It would seem to me, however, that the exposé, as it were, would better wait until after the election."

"But, Judge . . ."

"Hear me out. This is a very powerful man you're talking about. If you bring all this up now, it will just seem like a political smear. And it might smear me, too, because the same people who have endorsed the sheriff have endorsed me, and especially because of your involvement in my campaign. I just don't think this is the time."

"Well, I can't make any promises, Al. And I'm warning you to be careful around him so you don't get dragged under when he goes."

"If what you're saying is true, Tubby . . ." He held up his hand to stop the protest. "If what you say is true, it is you that should be careful. You're the one who could get dragged down. Thank you, doll," he smiled at the waitress serving more bread. "Could we have some more butter as well?"

"Some of the sheriff's cronies don't back you, Al, so that shouldn't be a major factor," Tubby argued. "I mean the sheriff has endorsed Carlo Trapani for criminal court judge, and Trapani is making ads for Benny Bloom."

The judge's face clouded. "That crook Trapani isn't fit to wear a robe. . . ."

"He's a crook?" Tubby asked.

"For enough money he'd let any child molester or mobster you can name out of jail." Hughes caught himself. "Now listen to me, repeating rumors. You got me sidetracked. I just don't think it's a good idea for the cochairman of my campaign to start slinging dirt at Sheriff Mulé the week before the election."

Tubby didn't answer. He was still thinking about what Judge Trapani could do for a minor mobster like Cesar Pitillero in exchange for the correct campaign contribution. If it was put to him just right.

Tubby also held nothing back in his attempt to persuade detective Fox Lane, N.O.P.D. Homicide, to mount an effort to bust Sheriff Mulé. He made reservations for two at Straya on St. Charles. He knew Fox loved a fancy spread. He even offered to pick her up, but she declined.

"I'm not sure where I'll be," she said. "Most likely outside of some bar taking pictures of a corpse."

That did not appear, however, to have been the case. She arrived, outfitted in a sleeveless black top embroidered in gold and dangling gold tassels over black leggings. Tubby had been shown to a booth facing the front and could see the eyes of other patrons following the six-feet-tall detective when she made her entrance. Tubby stood up to greet his guest. The waiter tagging behind her nodded his head with pleasure.

"You look great," the lawyer said admiringly. Fox was coffee-colored and from an old family, what New Orleans called Creole. Compliments had never bothered her.

"Hello, Counselor," she said with a smile that showed off a lot of white teeth. "You look pretty good yourself."

Indeed, Tubby had primped for the occasion. He was wearing a new summer seersucker he had just picked up at Perlis, and had gotten his hair cut that very afternoon by the barber in the Whitney Bank. He gallantly swept his arm across the table and invited her to join him.

The waiter asked what they might like to drink and pulled some menus from behind his back.

Fox ordered a glass of Merlot, Tubby an Old-fashioned.

"Ever been here before?" he asked.

"No, I've wanted to." She looked around at the palm trees and stars cut from brightly colored aluminum. "Reminds me of the World's Fair."

"Yeah, loud."

"Garish."

"Right, tacky."

"I like it."

"The menu has quite a few interesting things." He studied the list of salads with shrimp and crisp-fried crawfish, Crescent City wraps, and Baja stir-fried vegetables. If this didn't hook Fox, nothing would.

"Here's a dinner for two," he pointed out. "Barbecued shrimp and fettuccine with Creole seasonings and lemon-butter garlic, and an oyster Rockefeller pizza. Why don't we just get that?"

"That's a definite diet buster. What is it you want me to do, Tubby? Give up my job and run away to Nassau with you?"

"Would you?"

She smiled and accepted a glass of wine from the waiter. Tubby placed their order.

"You've gotta admire a place like this that is not afraid of doing something new, that has an aggressive spirit," Tubby began.

"Yeah, there are a bunch of new cops like that in my district. Real virile, who do push-ups for fun."

"I thought that described you."

"Not anymore." She swallowed some wine. "Nowadays I just try to get through, not break through. You were about to tell me what the occasion is for the dinner I'm about to enjoy."

"Let's just relax for a minute."

"Let me guess. This is to pay me back for all the times I've helped you out. And especially for saving you from the bank robbers in the French Quarter last Mardi Gras."

"You were great."

"So I'm right."

"Sure, I got a lot to thank you for, Fox, and there's something else I want to talk to you about."

Fox nodded. "Get it off your chest, big boy," she said.

"You know how, on that bank job, I kept saying there was someone else behind it, a bigger boss hiding in the woodwork—a crime czar."

"Crime czar," the policewoman repeated flatly. She fingered the stem of her wineglass and stared at the tablecloth.

"Yeah, and now I know who it is."

"Who, Tubby?"

Tubby leaned cross the table so that he would not be overheard by any nearby snoop.

"Sheriff Frank Mulé," he whispered.

The detective's eyes shot up to meet his.

"I'm afraid you've slipped a gear, old friend," she said softly.

"No, wait a minute. I've actually met with him. And you know who took me to the meeting?"

"Who?"

"A man named Willie LaRue. The one who you rescued me from. The one who shot Dan Haywood. The one you said burned up in a fire."

"I had a dead body," Fox said defensively. "But you say he's still alive?"

"Yes. We had breakfast together yesterday morning. Me, LaRue, and Mulé. At Shoney's, if you can believe that."

"You can identify this LaRue as the one who shot your friend?"

"Yes. Sure."

"Where is he. I'll pick him up myself."

"I don't want him picked up. LaRue doesn't count. It's the big boss who counts. Mulé."

"Tubby," Fox almost hissed across the table. "What is your evidence for saying these things about Sheriff Mulé? He's one of the most respected law enforcement officials in the parish."

"Respected or feared?"

"Both. What's your proof?"

"I'm going to get proof. I'm setting up a scam where I can get him to show his hand. Only thing is, I need up-front money to make it happen."

"What are you talking about?"

"I need a pretty big amount of money. Like half a million dollars."

"Now I know you're nuts."

"I know your department doesn't have that kind of money. But you know people in the FBI and the U.S. Attorney's office. That's probably small change for them. You could introduce me. Don't forget, this is your case."

"In no way, shape, or form is this my case. Now you forget that crap about half a million dollars. Tell me where to find LaRue. My job is to catch murderers."

"Fox, I won't tell you where LaRue is. Now let me explain my plan."

"I got dressed up for this?" She was indignant.

"I've got Mulé hooked on the idea of buying into a ladies' boxing franchise."

Fox stood up.

"I'm out of here," she said.

"Aw, come on. Wait! I knew we should have eaten first."

"You need to get some help, Tubby. Only I can't give it to you." She stood up, jammed her purse under her arm, and was gone.

Tubby, rising to follow her, met the waiter carrying a huge platter.

"Dinner for two?" he inquired, watching the front door wheeze shut.

"That's a lot of food," Tubby said.

He sat back down, looking at the oddest pizza he had ever met.

22

Judge Perez Highway got busier every year. Used to be when you took a trip to the parish you were in a world of fishing villages and truck farms as soon as you got past Arabi, but now it was all built up. Four-laned and cluttered with Wal-Marts and shopping centers, it was slow-going until you passed the sign, laced with bullet holes, that said you were entering Plaquemines Parish. Then the road narrowed, the tract housing gave way to house trailers and abundant piles of oil field equipment, and white egrets stood watching in any spot wet enough to hide a crawfish.

Tubby had the radio tuned to WWOZ, and Bobby "Blue" Bland howled from his open windows as the car whooshed down the straight highway. "Going to miss

my baby . . ." he was singing along, beating his hands
on the wheel. Gotta be pumped up to raise the big
bucks.

He was going to see Noel Parvelle, a man who had
made millions in the spice business. His garlic powder,
Cajun seasonings, hot pepper sauce, and gumbo herbs
were beside every cook's stove, though Parvelle had
long ago turned over management of the company that
bore his name to his sons. Now the old man sat around
thinking bitter thoughts and reading royalty statements
from all the oil wells he owned across southern
Louisiana.

Parvelle's driveway started at the blacktop by the
river levee, wound through a few acres of grassland
spotted with tall live oak and pecan trees under which
Brahman cattle grazed, and ended at a large house,
ringed by wide porches and raised about eight feet off
the ground on massive cypress posts. When hurricanes
blew through, a tidal swell from the Gulf of Mexico
might send waves of salty water over the lawn, but the
house was built to survive.

Parvelle was seated on his front porch, and he
watched Tubby park and climb the broad wooden steps.

"You're late," he barked.

"Sorry, Mr. Parvelle," Tubby said. "It took me more
time than I expected to drive through Chalmette. How
are you?" He offered the old man a hand to shake.

Parvelle was stuck in a wheelchair. He was no happier about it today than he was five years ago when a
high-speed drunken rampage over the levee in a Jeep

had put him there. He grabbed Tubby's hand and squeezed it like a hawk squeezes a rabbit's neck.

"Yo! Feeling pretty good, are you?"

"Have a seat!" Parvelle yelled. "What's your business?"

Tubby pulled an oak rocker up to the invalid's wheelchair and sat.

"You remember when you got ripped off in that oil lease sale back around Mardi Gras. When they got your counter-letter. When the Great Return Land and Investment Company was stolen from you? You told me you'd pay good money to know who was behind it all. Well, I know."

Parvelle just stared at him. His lips were stained with tobacco juice.

"I've got a plan to expose the son of a bitch," Tubby continued. "I just need a little money to make it work. I knew you'd want to be in on the deal."

Parvelle raised his head, showing off his knobby Adam's apple, and snorted. Spit hit his chin.

The guy is senile, Tubby thought.

"Mr. Parvelle. I've got the bad man in my sights. I need some cash though. You'll probably get your money back. I'm talking about the guy who set you up and stole your company from you. We can catch him."

"I know who it is," Parvelle sang, like a child in nursery school.

"What?" Tubby was confused. "You know who I am?"

"I know who he is," Parvelle sang again.

"You do?" Tubby wasn't going to get half a million dollars.

"Frank Mulé," Parvelle whispered loudly.

Tubby's jaw dropped open. All he could do was nod.

"I know everything you do, Mr. Lawyer."

"I guess you do," Tubby said. "Don't you want to catch him?"

"Why? Him and me are partners now. He said he was sorry for all the mix-up over the Great Return Investment Company. I told him I had a mind to break his legs, and he cut me in on the deal. We're great pals now."

"I wasn't expecting that," was all Tubby could think of to say.

"It's a cold world, son," Parvelle cackled. He squirted some brown syrup over the porch rail.

"Now I suppose you're going to tell the sheriff that I'm out to bust him."

"Not me, shyster. I don't owe that smelly little bastard the time of day. What happens to him happens. I got mine. You wanna get yours, that's your affair. But I don't owe you anything, either."

"What I had in mind was more along the lines of an investment."

"An investment in nailing Frank Mulé?" Parvelle laughed. "That's a loser, son. Get off of my porch."

The drive back to town seemed to take forever.

· · ·

Willie LaRue was stalled in traffic. He was trying to get on the bridge at St. Charles Avenue, and his path was blocked by a parade. From where he sat, it looked like some guy on a float dressed up like a crawfish with a lot of half-naked teenage girls dancing around him.

LaRue kept both hands on the wheel. His eyes blinked fast.

The sign on the float said, MONSTER MUDBUG FOR SHERIFF. The girls were pitching cups and doubloons at the startled bag ladies on the sidewalk.

Finally the mess cleared away and he could get onto the up-ramp. It was his day to visit his mom.

After parking at the Sweet Madonna Manor and checking in with the nurse, he took his customary seat across from the thin-faced old woman in her wheelchair.

"Willie here, Mom. Anybody home?"

He watched her eyes in vain for a sign of recognition.

"I guess you know I didn't turn out so well," he told her.

"Did you ever know it was me who killed Dad?

"No, I guess you didn't.

"Do you know what I do for a living?

"Do you know what pays the bills around here?"

LaRue looked at the ceiling. His eyes closed and he fell asleep.

When he woke up, his mother was staring at him. LaRue almost screamed, but he choked back the sound and composed himself quickly.

"Who gives a shit, anyway," he said, and he left. He had an errand to run.

He drove to the Original Babylonian Missionary Pentecostal Church on Telemachus Street. Another car was already in the lot, and a man was waiting patiently in the front seat. LaRue pulled into the next space. He got out of his car, and the man rolled down his window.

LaRue handed the man a thick envelope. "The sheriff said for me to give this to you personally," he said.

"Should I count it?" Benny Bloom asked.

"Not around me. I'm just the messenger boy."

LaRue turned on his heel and split.

23

Tubby was not accustomed to being treated like a lunatic. As a member in good standing of the Louisiana Bar, he could treat other people that way. But the title of lawyer was supposed to earn you a measure of respect—maybe even trepidation.

Driving under the expressway, where river-bound traffic was standing still and emergency vehicles, lights flashing, crowded the shoulders, Tubby thought maybe they were right.

Since he had fallen victim to this obsession, call it what you will, to get to the top of crime's ladder, he had not been much fun to be around. His daughters thought he was acting odd. He had even shrugged off Marguerite when she begged him to fly to Chicago. And it wasn't like there were lots of other women in his life.

But there was always the picture of Dan Haywood and the blood pulsing out of his chest to make him feel the anger again. He had a picture in his mind of Frank Mulé, lying in that same dirty gutter, staring sightless at the clouds while the life flowed red out of him. And there were those dreams he was having—all of those faces calling him, reaching for him. Tubby's fingers hurt so much from the way that he was gripping the steering wheel that he came back to the present and remembered to take his foot off the brake.

Tubby outlined his strategy to Flowers the next morning.

"Couldn't you have said a hundred thousand dollars rather than half a million?" was the detective's comment.

"Same difference," Tubby said. "I don't have either one."

"You know, I've heard rumors about a turf war between the downtown mobsters and the Vietnamese in New Orleans East," Flowers said. "I'm just thinking out loud, but maybe they'd be on our side."

"You mean Bin Minny?"

"Yeah."

"I've never met him. I've seen his picture in the papers. You reckon he would talk to me?"

"He's got a restaurant."

Thus, Flowers and Tubby drove out of town for lunch at the Empress of Saigon.

A woman with long black eyelashes and ruby-red lips, who could have been fifteen or thirty, showed them to a table in a dark corner. A huge aquarium dominated the far wall, and they could watch schools of fish flit about in a brilliant blue bubbling sea as much as they cared to.

"If Mr. Minh is in, would you please give him my card?" Tubby laid one gently in the waitress's palm. "You could tell him that I desire to speak about an important subject."

She accepted the card wordlessly. With feet concealed by a tight silk dress, she seemed to blow away on a scented breeze.

Flowers fidgeted with his menu and stared restlessly around the room. He gave a second glance to the only other diners, a pair of muscular youths quietly eating bowls of noodles by the front window.

They looked up, as did Tubby, when a tall, thin man, neat black hair to match his suit, emerged from behind a partition and followed the slender waitress to the newcomers' table.

She stood aside politely, as if reluctant to mention his name. The proprietor introduced himself.

"I am Mr. Minh. I hope you are enjoying yourself in my establishment." His voice purred.

"We've just arrived. I wonder, Mr. Minh, if you might join us just for a moment and let me explain an important proposition."

"I am afraid, gentlemen, that I already have all of the insurance I need, and I have no plans to invest in a mutual fund."

"I'm not selling anything, Mr. Minh. I'm giving it away, and I only want a minute of your time."

"Certainly," Minh said and gracefully took a chair. "Chi Lamb, please see what these gentlemen would like to drink."

"Tea," said Tubby.

"Same for me," Flowers said.

Bin Minny shook his head slightly, and the waitress floated off.

"It's like this," Tubby began. "I'm a lawyer, and I've been making it my business to know the leading criminal element in New Orleans."

Bin Minny's head jerked to attention and his eyes narrowed.

"My purpose has been partly curiosity," Tubby continued. "I wanted to know how things were organized and, naturally, who was the chairman of the board. But it's more than that. Friends of mine have been killed, so I want to see the killers, by which I mean the top dog, brought to justice."

"What does that have to do with me?" Bin Minny asked, wary and perplexed.

"My research has paid off," Tubby explained. "I now know the name of the man pulling the strings, and I have a plan to punish him. However, I need allies. It has been rumored that you also may have reason to oppose this man. I've heard he may be trying to take over your territory. Perhaps it would be in your interest to help me."

"Who are you?" Mr. Minh's question was directed at Flowers.

"He's a private detective who works for me," Tubby answered.

This was not reassuring to Bin Minny. "What is the name of this boss of whom you are speaking?" he asked.

"He's a powerful elected official. He keeps lots of people in jail."

"Yes. I was thinking of that same man," Bin Minny said. "He has some butchers working for him."

"I've met at least one. His name is Willie LaRue. They call him Rue."

"Rue. I don't know that name, but I will find out about him."

"Then you will help me trap these people?"

"How could I help?"

"My plan sounds a little complicated at first. You see, I have invented a false business opportunity, and I'm going to talk the boss into investing. It will take seed money, and that's another thing I need to ask you about. But inevitably, we will expose the boss and his key people."

"And then what happens?"

"Hopefully they will go to jail for a long time."

Bin Minny dismissed the whole conversation with a wave of his hand.

"Not a very satisfactory ambition," he announced, and stood up. He bowed stiffly from the waist.

"Thank you for taking me away from my boring office, and thank you for your information. There is nothing I can do for you."

"Please, wait," Tubby implored, but he was talking to the owner's back. Then Bin Minny was gone.

"Bummer," Flowers said. "You want to get some sushi?"

"Hell no," Tubby said, and pulled on his coat.

24

Flowers had learned how to "half sleep." The idea was to relax the body and let the mind go blank. Slow down the breathing, but don't let the eyelids shut. That's what he was doing, way past midnight, slumped behind the steering wheel of a dingy gray van parked down the street from LaRue's mother's house in Harvey. If he had stirred to check his watch, he would have seen that he had been there about two hours.

So far, two anonymous late-model cars had crossed his line of vision and proceeded harmlessly down the street. A pickup truck with a hole in its muffler had growled past. A cat had crossed the street. A dog locked up behind the bars of the welding shop had barked for a long time. There had been no sign of LaRue.

Flowers was thinking about nothing when the corner of his eye caught a shadow moving across the street.

Someone had entered the LaRues' small and untidy front yard and was hiding behind the large tree growing there. The shadow moved again, into a narrow alley beside the house.

Quietly, the detective opened the door of his van and slid down to the sidewalk. Keeping the tree between himself and the alleyway, he moved catlike across the street.

The grass on the lawn was tall and wet. Flowers crept stealthily to the corner of the silent residence and peered around it. Someone was on the other side of a pair of trash cans trying the side door to the house. He heard the rattle of the knob, but the attempt to enter was unsuccessful. That door was locked. Flowers had already checked that.

The figure backed away and turned toward the rear of the building.

"Hrumph." Flowers coughed.

The person jumped in surprise and then crouched down to hide.

"All of the doors are locked," Flowers said. His voice was soft, but it carried clearly down the dark alley. "Come out and let's see who you are."

"I'm armed," a woman's voice said. Flowers had to think for a second, but then it came to him.

"Is that you, Daisy?" he asked. "This is Flowers. We met at the bar."

"Bad karma," she said and stood up.

"You're not going to shoot me, are you?" Flowers asked.

"I ought to," she said and marched up to face him. She was wearing a black sweater, black jeans, and a purple scarf over her hair.

"LaRue's not here," Flowers whispered.

"I figured that out, asshole." Daisy pushed past him.

Flowers grabbed her arm. She tried to jerk it back, but he held tight.

"We're trying to keep an eye on him, lady. You sneaking around, you're liable to get hurt, or even worse, scare him away."

"You mind your own business. And let go of my arm!" This time she got it loose.

"Fuck off," she called over her shoulder as she walked away.

Flowers watched Daisy go down the street and wondered where she had parked her car, or if she even had a car. He thought about following her but decided against it. In any case, this particular stakeout was shot.

Driving away, he turned on a Latin station he favored and tried to figure out how he would spend the remaining hours until dawn.

Tubby had been trying to maintain his sobriety, but that's hard to do sitting in a bar drinking with a friend. Especially when you owned the bar, and when the friend had a dissolute personality.

"It's a corrupt town, that's all there is to it," Tubby griped.

Raisin shrugged. Suddenly he pointed to the television set hanging above the bar in the corner. "Hey, look at that!"

On the screen a train was derailing, its passengers hurdling about the cars and flying out of the windows. Many lay writhing in agony on stony ground. As emergency rescue crews fought to get to the scene, a helicopter appeared overhead and a man dangling from it by a rope—a man in a three-piece suit who looked just like Benny Bloom—screamed "Let me sign you up!"

"Benny Bloom signed up seven hundred and eighty-three plaintiffs at the Pearl River train derailment," the announcer said solemnly.

Then an oil refinery blew up. The same lawyer crawled over the bodies of fallen workers, stepping on hard hats, begging, "Let me sign you up!"

"Benny Bloom signed up one hundred and forty-six so-called plaintiffs at the Ratco fire," the announcer said.

An ambulance raced down a busy highway, lights flashing. Benny Bloom ran behind it waving his briefcase and crying, "Let me sign you up!"

"Do you want an ambulance chaser for judge?" the sober voice asked.

"That's pretty good," Tubby said, watching the face of Al Hughes smile down from the bench.

Raisin laughed soundlessly.

"Just shows you, this is a corrupt town," Tubby repeated, returning to his theme. "Here we got a sheriff who runs a major crime syndicate, who whacks people out with impunity, and who eats at Shoney's, for God's sake."

Raisin signaled the bartender and tapped his glass for more.

"And nobody wants to do anything about it. Not even people he's screwed in the past . . ."

Larry, the barkeep, drifted over to place fresh glasses, already full of whiskey, in front of them both.

"Not even the police, such as my so-called friend Detective Fox Lane. Not even that crazy Vietnamese. Not even my own goddamn judge." Tubby slapped the bar and grabbed his glass. He tossed it back.

"What do you think about that?" he asked hoarsely.

"Not a damn thing," Raisin muttered.

"Well that's not very helpful, is it?"

"I'll be honest with you, good buddy," Raisin said. "I think everybody's getting a little bit sick and tired of hearing about your crime czar." He sipped from his own cup and checked his appearance in the speckled, cloudy mirror behind the bar.

Tubby for once was speechless.

Raisin searched around for his pack of cigarettes.

"Tired of hearing about it?" Tubby finally managed.

"Crime boss, crime boss. Tubby, who really gives a wad of spit?"

Tubby was having trouble processing this betrayal by his best friend. The room, it seemed, was rotating. Had everyone deserted him? He failed to hear the knock on the tavern's front door, and he did not notice Larry pressing the buzzer that would admit a new patron.

"I really don't know what to say," he finally mumbled.

"How about 'hello'?" the lady behind him suggested.

"Marguerite!" Tubby exclaimed. He turned to find his most recent old flame, all five-feet-six of her, beaming her blue eyes at him.

Awkwardly, they embraced.

"I thought I would surprise you," she said.

"Man, you sure did. Raisin Partlow, this is my friend Marguerite Patino I told you about."

Raisin sized her up. "Pleased to meet you," he said. Marguerite was easy to look at—nice plump shape, straw-colored hair, black eyelashes. Tubby moved aside to give her a stool between the two men at the bar.

"Are you in town for long?" he asked.

"Maybe," she said. "I just, you know, wanted to see New Orleans again. I called you when I got here this afternoon but, of course, you weren't home. So I went out and had a bad dinner. Then I remembered you had told me about Mike's Bar, and, well, I just took a chance. And here you are."

"Here I am," Tubby admitted.

"Just in time," Raisin said happily.

"I hope we'll have a chance to have some fun," she said hopefully.

"You bet," Tubby said. "There's a lot going on with me right now, but I can make some time."

Marguerite did not seem to mind that Tubby was already a little cross-eyed. She fanned Raisin's smoke out of her eyes and ordered a glass of wine.

Larry displayed the wine menu at Mike's—both the white and the red selections came with screw-off caps—and she decided on a light beer instead.

She and Tubby talked and started nudging and patting each other. Raisin finally got bored.

"It's getting late," he said. "I guess I'll head out."

"Hey, it's early," Tubby protested.

"I don't feel tired," Marguerite said.

Raisin could take a hint and split anyway.

"You want to go hear some music?" Tubby suggested. He had only the faintest idea where to catch a band at that time of the night. It had been years since he had thought about looking for one.

"I'd rather go someplace quiet and maybe have a cup of coffee and talk."

"Sounds good to me." He was relieved.

Larry condescended to give them a nod when they walked out the door.

"He's a funny guy," Marguerite noted. "Does he ever talk?"

"Every few years he'll have something to say. If he likes you. Do you have a car?"

No, she had arrived in a cab. So they piled into Tubby's Chrysler. He thought she smelled really nice.

"Let's see," he said, starting the engine. The clock on the dashboard said 1:14. "Coffee."

"I guess not many places are open."

"Maybe at your hotel. Where are you staying?"

"A guest house on the streetcar line called the Parkview."

"Really, that's close to my house. But I don't think their kitchen will be open this late."

"Well, haven't you got a coffeepot?"

Sure he did, and so Tubby took her to his house.

"Nice place," she remarked when he let her in the front door.

"Thanks," he said. He was just glad none of his kids had picked this night to hang around.

They sat in the kitchen and decided on a bottle of Château Ste. Michelle rather than a cup of coffee.

Marguerite told what she had been doing for the past few months, since her hurried departure from New Orleans with a sack of stolen jewelry.

She had succeeded in converting a portion of her wealth into conventional assets, including a condominium overlooking Lake Michigan and substantial holdings in tax-free municipal bonds. She had quit her job as a flunky for a commodities trader and pursued some personal interests. She had, for example, learned to cook—Chicago-style—and taken a couple of trips. She had gone to Vail, Colorado, to ski. Now she had come to New Orleans to see what the city looked like when it wasn't raining. And to see Tubby, of course.

Tubby brought her up to date on the happenings in his life, the birth of a grandson, Dan Haywood's death, and his search for the crime czar. His eyes shone brightly when he talked about that.

"I can see it means a lot to you," she said.

"I think it's the most important thing for me to do," he explained. "And I believe I've built a good trap for him."

"But you're short on bait," she pointed out.

He nodded.

"Then I'll help," Marguerite said. "I'm rich."

"You would do that?"

"Sure. It's an investment. I'll get my money back, right?"

"That's the idea, but it's obviously very risky."

"If I'm going to put my money in I want to know everything that's going on."

"Don't worry. I'll tell you everything I do."

"That's not what I mean, Tubby. I want to be there when it happens."

"It's way too dangerous. These people are killers."

"Take it or leave it. I'm the kind of woman who keeps a close watch on her dough." She had, in fact, a nice little stash of some of her favorite priceless items in the hotel safe.

"Now, come on . . ."

"No. You come on."

They went upstairs to the guest room bed.

They were just getting comfortable when the telephone rang. Thinking it might be one of his daughters calling so late at night, Tubby picked up the receiver.

"I just want to know," Daisy said, "did you nail the son of a bitch yet?" Her voice was loud. She was drunk.

"Meaning who?"

"The so-called sheriff."

"How do you know anything about Sheriff Mulé?"

"I hear things in my line of work," Daisy said. "It doesn't take a genius."

One could take offense at that, Tubby thought. "Well, keep it quiet," he begged her. "It looks like I'm getting close, Daisy. Very close."

"And when you get there, what the hell happens to him?"

"He loses a lot of money. That's what really hurts a guy like him."

"Will it cost him his job?"

"Maybe . . ."

"Will it cost him his life?" Her voice was rising. She was getting hysterical.

"I doubt that, but he might go to jail. If that happened he might very well be in danger."

"Maybe isn't good enough."

"Well, I'm taking my best shot."

"All legal and nice, is that it?"

"That's right. You can't take the law into your own hands. You've got to use the law, but use it for your own purposes, and . . ."

She hung up.

Tubby rolled over to look at Marguerite.

"That's what you think?" she asked. "You use the law for your own purposes?"

"What's wrong with that?"

"Nothing, but I thought you were supposed to have higher standards."

"Do you? You flew out of New Orleans with a million dollars' worth of other people's jewelry."

"It was more than a million, and I never said I was perfect. I don't have to justify myself. Do you?"

Do I? Tubby wondered.

She ran her hand down his stomach and he forgot the question.

Daisy composed her face in the mirror and went back to the party in the hotel suite. The red, white, and blue banners hanging from the walls read BLOOM FOR JUDGE. A MAN YOU CAN TRUST.

25

The street in front of Swan's Gym was deserted at night, except for a gray cat on the prowl for food. Overhead, the ramp to the Crescent City Connection droned with a steady stream of cars. It was bright up there, dark down here.

A polished black Cadillac rolled slowly down Erato Street. It bumped gently over the curb and came to a stop on the sidewalk in front of the gymnasium. Sheriff Mulé's henchmen got out as a group. A large man whose name was Courtney went swiftly to the dented steel door and pushed it open. A bolt of light escaped. Skinny Willard LaRue escorted the sheriff inside. The driver, Shakes, stayed with the car.

Tubby was leaning against the ring, distractedly

watching Denise DiMaggio, known as the "Bayou Babe," spar lightly with "Black Velvet," late of St. Gabrielle. He had been worried that Mulé might not show up. Marguerite sat on one of the cracked wooden theater seats, eyes fixed on the fighters. The lawyer turned when he heard the door open and hurried forward to greet the short sheriff and his entourage.

"This is your million dollar operation?" Mulé asked, not pausing to shake hands.

"Wait till you see the action," Tubby promised. "Here, get yourself a drink."

He prodded the sheriff to a makeshift bar beside a red punching bag. Here, where the fighters' 10-K and water bottles were usually stored, Tubby had arrayed a half dozen fifths of whiskey and a bucket of ice. The dashing dark-haired man tending bar was Flowers. LaRue recognized the detective and stopped short. Flowers grinned at him.

"What will it be, gentlemen?" he asked.

"Scotch and a splash," Mulé grunted. "You guys get whatever you want," he told Courtney and LaRue. He glared around the room. All of the lights were pointed into the ring where Denise, tight black shorts over a cobalt-blue bodysuit, was prancing around Velvet, who was outfitted in purple tights cut low at the top and high at the bottom.

Mulé took his drink without turning his gaze from the boxers. Tubby grabbed a bourbon and told LaRue to help himself. He guided the sheriff over to the seats.

"Relax, Sheriff. When we go big time you won't be able to have a private exhibition like this. Unless you're one of the owners, of course. Let me introduce you to my friend. Marguerite, this is our high sheriff, Frank Mulé."

"Pleased to meetcha," Mulé said, sitting down heavily next to her. He quickly returned his attention to the ring.

"Same here," Marguerite said, a little annoyed.

LaRue crossed the room and took a seat behind them. Courtney, one hand wrapped in a bandage, stayed at the bar, passing wisecracks with Flowers.

LaRue leaned over and whispered in his boss's ear, "I know the broad beside you."

Mulé shrugged.

"Let's see some action," Tubby suggested loudly.

Flowers jerked a chain and rang the bell.

Denise and Black Velvet came out of their corners, and without much preamble, started slugging each other.

"Ugh!" Denise grunted when a padded scarlet fist caught her in the stomach.

"Oh!" Velvet cried when a quick uppercut found her left eye.

Tubby had to count the holes in the ceiling tiles, as he often did when attending such sporting events. Mulé, on the other hand, watched intently, a crooked grin on his face, grinding one large fist into the palm of his other hand.

"Quite a show," Marguerite said.

"You betcha!" Mulé replied.

Velvet went down on her knees in the third round and couldn't get up. Denise jumped around her energetically, burning off adrenaline. Flowers bounded into the ring and called the fight.

"The winner by a knockout is the knockout Bayou Babe!" he proclaimed, holding her red-gloved hand in the air.

The victor made a few turns around the ring to vent her attitude and then helped her partner get back on her feet. Flowers parted the ropes so that the boxers could climb out. Velvet headed for the showers, but Denise slipped over to give Tubby a sweaty hug.

"I sure recognize you, Sheriff," she said throatily, and gave him a hug, too. "We're so glad you could watch our show."

"Sweetheart, it was great." Mulé couldn't take his eyes off her chest.

"You can come anytime," she said. Denise gave him a cute wave, while Tubby cringed, and ran back to the locker room.

"Put this in a quality facility and you'll sell out every night," Tubby said enthusiastically. "You won't be able to keep network television away."

"Maybe," Mulé said, eyes glistening. Tubby knew he was sold.

"Tell me again how much investment we're talking here," Mulé said.

"I put up five hundred thousand, you put up five hundred thousand," Tubby said.

"Where would a two-bit lawyer like you get cash like that?" Mulé was glaring again.

Tubby pointed to Marguerite.

From underneath her seat she pulled a large black leather handbag. She put it in her lap, smiled, and unsnapped the clasp. Her hand went inside and came out with a fistful of diamond bracelets and gold chains.

"Holy shit!" the sheriff exclaimed.

"That stuff's mine. It's from the First Alluvial Bank job," LaRue cried. He made a grab for her hand but was restrained by an arm around his neck that belonged to Flowers. LaRue was slammed back into his chair. Across the room, Courtney was arm-wrestling with Denise.

The sheriff never took his eyes away from the sparkling jewels.

"Nice bracelet," he said, pointing to a heavy gold chain with man-sized links.

"That's our investment," Tubby said.

"It's hot," the sheriff pointed out.

"That's a small problem," Tubby agreed. "That's why I brought this deal to you. Isn't this something you could handle?"

"I suppose," Mulé said thoughtfully. "There's a big discount on this kind of investment, you know."

"Yeah, I know," Tubby said. "Here's an inventory of what we're putting up. It's all listed out—by carats.

Very neat." He dropped the paper into the sheriff's hand. "Retail market value is about three million," he added.

Mulé stood up. "You'll be hearing from my lawyers." He waved at Denise. "My compliments to the ladies. Come on boys, let's go."

26

Clifford Banks was a Garden District lawyer. His specialties were mortgage authority bonds and mixed doubles at the New Orleans Tennis Club. His straight and narrow course rarely crossed Tubby's errant path. It was surprising, therefore, when Cherrylynn buzzed the lawyer's inner office and announced that Clifford Banks was on the phone.

"Good morning, Counselor," Tubby said cautiously.

"Good morning, Tubby. How's the legal game?" They exchanged pleasantries and agreed that the day had been hot.

"The reason I'm calling," Banks finally said, "is that Frank Mulé asked me to. I help him with some of his business interests—though he's got a lot I don't know about . . .."—Banks chuckled—"and he has asked me to arrange a meeting with you to discuss a particularly fascinating proposal that, I understand, involves beautiful female prizefighters." Banks laughed out loud at that.

"Frank told me his lawyer would call." Tubby put his feet up on his desk and looked out the window. "I just didn't know who the lawyer would be."

"Fine, then I'm sure you have a good picture of what's going on. Better than I have, probably. Frank doesn't always fill me in on a lot of details. But he would like us to get together and jawbone as soon as possible. Perhaps tomorrow."

"You and me?"

"You, me, and Frank, actually."

"Would you like to come to my office?"

"Truthfully, Frank would like to meet at his."

"At the jail?"

"I'm afraid so. That's where a lawman feels most secure, I guess." Ha ha.

"I'm bringing my principal."

"You're what?"

"My principal investor. My client."

"Ah, and who might that be?"

"Mulé has met her. You will soon."

Banks didn't like it, but he took it. They settled upon ten o'clock the next morning as the optimum time.

• • •

It was a long night for Tubby. The reality of what he was getting into was beginning to penetrate. Touching Sheriff Mulé had burned braver men than this lawyer, he was sure. He could almost feel the dark waters of the Mississippi River closing over his head. It's something I've got to do, he told himself. Beside the flickering lamp at his bedside, he composed a letter to his daughters. Sensing his mood, Marguerite left him alone.

It was also a long night for Benny Bloom. He had seen a poll showing that he was trailing Al Hughes by five points. Even worse, a certain judge to whom he had offered a certain envelope had handed it back, saying things were "too sensitive"—meaning he was worried about his skin. The prospect of losing the election did not really bother him. The prospect of losing a big money case, on the other hand, did.

Tubby arrived with Marguerite at the jail a few minutes ahead of schedule.

"What if he locks us in?" she whispered as they trudged up the concrete steps. She was enjoying this.

"Don't joke. He might do it," Tubby replied.

The automatic doors slid open.

Usually, Tubby found whatever guard confronted

him at the main desk to be surly and uncooperative, but today was different.

"Right this way," the beefy, black-uniformed deputy said as soon as they introduced themselves. "You can go up in the sheriff's elevator."

They were shown to the private car, which had only one button, for the fifth floor. The elevator itself was as dingy as the rest of the place. The surprise was that it opened onto a sumptuous suite of offices—superior, in fact, to Tubby's own.

An attractive woman, blond hair in striking contrast to her jet-black uniform and polished boots, greeted them suspiciously. She would let the sheriff know they were there.

Tubby sat on a leather-covered armchair while Marguerite paced around examining the odd oil paintings of jungle animals devouring one another. An enormous tiger clawing a terrified gazelle seemed particularly to engage her attention. She turned to ask Tubby a question, but just then the deputy's intercom buzzed and they were told to walk right in to the sheriff's private den.

Mulé's office was approximately the size of a basketball court and his handsome desk the size of a billiard table. Sitting behind it, the sheriff seemed more like a paperweight than the master of the manse, until he opened his mouth and started giving orders.

"Take yourself a seat right next to my lawyer," he barked. Banks, tall with graying temples and a pocket handkerchief, stood to greet them.

Tubby introduced Ms. Patino to the men and held her chair while she got situated. The stuffed head of an ibex glared down at them from the wall.

"Let's get right to the pernt," Mulé shouted. "Dubonnet here says he has the exclusive on a franchise for women's boxing in New Orleans, and he wants me to invest. I'm interested, and I've got my lawyer here to see that everything's on the up and up. Now how does Ms. Patino fit into things?" He fixed his beady eyes on the only woman in the room.

"She's my main organizer . . . ," Tubby began.

"I'm the one who has possession of the, uh, riches," Marguerite said, holding Mulé's stare.

"All right then," the sheriff announced. "Now we got the players straight. Who's the franchise from?"

"The WWB," Tubby said. "Worldwide Women's Boxing. They sanction the fights at the Coconut Casino, the Hot Slot, all the boats. Now they're expanding, backed by television contracts. They're planning to build twenty-five arenas around the country over the next two years. New Orleans is ours for the asking."

"Now how much money did you say this could earn?"

Tubby faithfully repeated the projections he had made up at the restaurant.

"I assume you've got all of this laid out on paper?" Banks asked.

"Of course." Tubby pulled a stack of documents from his briefcase. He and Marguerite had spent most of the previous day manufacturing a fake prospectus, with help from Cherrylynn and her word processor.

"Give all that to Banks," Mulé directed. "He can look at all of it later. Let's talk about the money you want."

"You've seen what we have," Tubby said. "I'm ready to put it up just as soon as you do the same."

"Who's gonna hold it?" Mulé wanted to know.

"We would open a joint bank account," Banks interjected.

"That won't work, at least not right away," Tubby said. "Our investment isn't entirely liquid."

Mulé nodded understandingly.

"However," Tubby told Banks, "if the sheriff puts up cash I see no reason why you couldn't hold his money as well as our loot, I mean investment, as an escrow agent, so to speak. At least until Frank can convert our investment into dollars. I would accept your word, Counselor, that you would hold the stakes of both parties in trust and keep everything safe."

"Why, of course I would," Banks murmured, eyes closed.

The sheriff smiled just like he did in his Mardi Gras ad.

"And," Tubby continued, "we can create a company. It won't take me or Clifford long. Let's say we call it 'Mission Enterprises.' "

Banks nodded his assent.

"So, where's the dough?" Mulé asked.

"I'll bring it to Mr. Banks's office myself," Marguerite said, "since Tubby trusts him so implicitly." She patted her lawyer's knee. "Where's your dough, Sheriff?"

Mulé pulled open the top drawer of his desk and brought out a yellow check. He looked at it lovingly for a moment before displaying it for the others to see. It was a certified check for five hundred thousand dollars, drawn on the Whiteside Bank, made payable to cash.

"That certainly looks negotiable," Tubby said appreciatively.

"I wouldn't normally use a check like this," Mulé said, "but I know it will be safe with Clifford." He eyed his lawyer carefully.

"Ahem, why certainly, Sheriff." Banks reached for the check and slipped it inside his coat. "Perfectly safe," he added.

"Don't lose it," Tubby said.

"Because it's the same as cash," the sheriff added.

"My law firm is quite safe," Banks told them.

"Enough said. My partner and I will come by your office tomorrow morning," Tubby promised, "and bring you our contribution. I'd say this afternoon, but I've got an 'Al Hughes for Judge' crawfish boil going on in my backyard."

"Oh, yeah? I might come to that," Mulé said. "It's always good to press the flesh."

27

Rolling Sam had the nicest table at the Empress of Saigon Restaurant, right beside the fish tank. And he had the most glamorous company—two sisters, Song and Wran, who sat on either side of him and laughed at his jokes.

Sam always went first-class, especially at Bin Minny's restaurant, where he could run a tab.

So tonight they were enjoying bun tom, laque duck, and shrimp on sugarcane.

The bun tom had just been served when a shadow fell across the table. Rolling Sam looked up to see Bin Minny looming over the diners.

"Good evening, Sam," Bin Minny said politely.

"I am pleased that you and your beautiful companions have selected my restaurant for your enjoyable meal."

"Hi, Mr. Minh. The food is truly wonderful tonight. This is Song and this is Wran."

Minh bowed slightly. "So nice to meet you," he said. "Now I must have a word with Rolling Sam, and I reluctantly ask the ladies to excuse us for a few minutes."

Song and Wran smiled and looked blankly at each other.

"Go to the powder room, girls," Rolling Sam explained.

The two did as instructed, and Bin Minny took a chair next to Sam's.

"Tell me what you have found out," he said.

"The 'short man' is not such an easy target," Rolling Sam reported. "There is a bodyguard who travels with him and who lives with him at his home."

"The 'short man' is not married?" Bin Minny inquired.

"No, sir, he is not. But the house presents problems. It is on a private street, very exclusive, and there is a guardhouse where all cars must stop. His bodyguard drives him to and from work."

"How about at the jail?"

"We have people in the jail," Rolling Sam whispered, "but unfortunately they do not have access to his office. The sheriff avoids going into the cell blocks."

"He is campaigning for reelection. A political event

where he appears in public might provide you with the best opportunity."

"Well, sure, but there are naturally going to be a lot of people around. It might almost require a suicide attack to reach him."

"Absolutely not," Bin Minny hissed. "We are not Japanese. Whoever accomplishes this hit will be rewarded, but he will be rewarded even more if he escapes." And the sooner the better, Bin Minny thought. He was beginning to have nighttime visions of corpses lined up, as if at the railing of a ship, singing, reaching for him with bony fingers, screaming for peace. Their visits had frightened him more than any of his living enemies ever had. This unfinished business must be attended to.

Rolling Sam bowed his head.

"I think we can get him soon," he said softly.

"That is what I want," Bin Minny said. "Now I'll go back to work, and your lady friends can come back and enjoy their meal. Please don't get up."

The boss went away to greet his customers and count his money.

The sky was blue, the afternoon breezy, and the aroma of boiling crawfish filled Tubby's backyard and made his guests' eyes water. Two huge aluminum pots, heated by jets of propane, were being tended at the same time by Raisin Partlow, whom Tubby had forgiven for his insulting attitude at the bar.

The host himself was clad in Banana Republic shorts and a luau shirt and was passing out beer while his two younger daughters, Christine and Colette, circulated with trays of steamed mushrooms, garlic potatoes, chips, and dips. Two picnic tables had been pulled together and covered with newspapers to hold the mounds of hot, spicy crawfish that would soon be ready.

The turnout was respectable—for a fund-raising party. Many noteworthies of the local Bar had come to show their support for Judge Hughes and to get a free meal. Jacob Solomon was there, spinning yarns about the tarpon fishing at Grand Isle. Ponder Fitzpugh was giving a lecture on the Saints defensive line. Carmelite Mirabelle was laughing about the federal judge who told her at a sidebar conference to loosen her jockstrap.

Judge Hughes was at the center of things, shaking hands with one and all. Marguerite was by Tubby's side, accepting compliments, and all was right with the world.

"Would you like some cheese and crackers?" Christine asked Marguerite. Tubby drifted away.

"Why, thank you. Now let's see. You're Tubby's middle child, is that right?"

"Uh-huh," Christine nodded. "You're from Chicago, and you met my father last Mardi Gras when it flooded, right?"

"That's what happened," Marguerite said, stuffing a cracker into her mouth.

"I bet you don't like New Orleans."

"Why do you say that? I like it very much."

"I just think we're so undisciplined here, the way people party all the time."

"Well, I don't think you party all the time, do you? But this is certainly a lot of fun."

"I guess it is, if you've never done it before. Have you ever eaten crawfish?"

"No, and I'm a little afraid to try."

"There's a trick to it. I'll be glad to show you when they're ready."

"Would you? Thanks."

"Okay. I'll be back." Christine was gone with her tray.

"Are you doing okay?" Tubby asked over his shoulder.

"I think I passed the first test," Marguerite said.

"It's a nice party," a voice behind them said.

Tubby turned to find Clifford Banks.

"Why hello, Cliff. I didn't realize that you supported Al Hughes or I would have invited you earlier."

"Surely I support him. I think he's done an outstanding job as judge."

"Help yourself to a beer."

"Thanks. Frank Mulé may be over in a while."

"Great. The more the merrier," was what Tubby said, but lie down with dogs, you wake up with fleas was what he was thinking. He looked across the yard and was startled to see Daisy saunter through the gate. That woman turns up everywhere, he thought to himself. Daisy looked relatively demure in pink sneakers, black tights, and a purple sweatshirt that matched her socks. She glanced toward the host, tossed her head in greeting, and melted into the crowd.

Raisin and a hefty neighbor named Parker O'Malley parted the sea of people, lugging between them the first of the steaming pots. With a heave-ho they upended it over the picnic tables and a huge pile of bright red crawfish poured over the newspaper.

Tubby noted a trio of Asians entering through the gate. They were similarly dressed in loose white shirts and black slacks, and all were hidden behind sunglasses.

Must be Republicans, Tubby thought, dismissing them as yet another beaming barrister pumped his hand.

Above the gentle hubbub of the party, the guests began to notice the loud wail and throbbing musical beat of "Chain, Chain, Chain."

"Some fool with his super-blaster cranked up, cruising for chicks in the neighborhood," was Tubby's first guess.

Up the block, dogs started to howl.

The music grew in intensity and conversation became difficult.

Raisin looked with some concern at his turkey pot, propane turned up full blast, which was vibrating dangerously on its iron stand.

To the mortification of the host, the image that appeared at the wide-open gate of his yard was a familiar self-propelled carnival float, draped in seaweed and equipped with four generator-driven Bose speakers, known as the Monster Mobile. On its hood, extremely young ladies dressed as immodest mermaids hopped up and down to the deafening music and lobbed beads as the guests covered their ears with their hands. Above them, stirring a huge fake cook pot, was the world's largest imitation crustacean, Monster Mudbug himself, outfitted in his trademark shiny red shell.

The vehicle lurched into the yard and joined the fun. Tubby's guests stepped lively to avoid being run down and crushed beneath the slow-moving carriage, which carried a big sign proclaiming MONSTER MUDBUG FOR SHERIFF—TAKE A BITE OUT OF CRIME.

While the candidate's true face was concealed within a pointy plastic head, there was no mistaking his glee. He waved wildly at Tubby and hurled stacks of cups into the air.

Tubby's yard, while substantial by neighborhood standards, was not designed for parades. His invitees were stumbling into each other trying to avoid the unstable float that was attempting a slow circuit of the estate. Between the mermaids' dancing legs, Tubby got a glimpse of the driver—a kid with mirror-blue sunglasses and a Zephyrs cap on backward who might have been the Monster's nephew Roger.

Misjudging the location of his papier-mâché fender, Roger nudged into the table supporting the steaming piles of crawfish.

Crying out in unintelligible protest, Raisin bolted across the yard to grab a corner of the table, saving the entire feast from sliding onto the grass. He screamed for help but could not be heard in the general pandemonium.

Nor, as the unguided elephant upended several recently occupied lawn chairs, did anyone have the presence of mind to kill the fire under the frying turkey. In a flash, the aluminum pot full of roiling peanut oil was engulfed in flames. The pot itself began to melt.

"I'll be damned," Raisin said to anyone who cared to listen. "I didn't know it would do that."

Daisy, who had taken refuge between the pot and Tubby's wooden fence, was in danger of being incinerated. She screamed. Noticing her plight, Monster Mudbug reached down with his horny claw and scooped her up into the float.

"You're crazy!" Daisy shrieked at his mandibles.

"Don't say that. It's not my fault," the Monster pleaded, frantically trying to get his nephew to reverse direction and exit the yard.

Meanwhile the peanut oil fire was threatening to take out Tubby's fig tree. He could see his neighbor tapping on her window and pointing at the flames flickering up her fence.

He fought his way through his guests, who were now departing en masse, to get to his telephone inside the house.

Without loosening his grip on Daisy, Monster Mudbug kicked his nephew away from the wheel and clumsily steered his booming machine back out to the street. He waved a feeble farewell.

Raisin watched his carefully prepared meal come to a spectacularly disastrous conclusion.

"Nuts," he said and let the table fall. An avalanche of crawfish washed over the grass.

And, as it turned out, Sheriff Mulé was a no-show.

28

The machine talking into Tubby's ear said that this was a collect call from the Orleans Parish Prison. The charges were fifty cents per minute. To accept, press 1.

"Hi, Tubby, it's me."

"Hey, Cesar. What's going on?"

"I called you to find out. I haven't heard from you."

"Nothing much to report," the lawyer said guiltily. "I've been busy."

"Oh, okay." Cesar's voice cracked. "Sure, okay."

"But I'm working on it."

"Work fast if you can. I can't sleep. These guys play dominoes all night, and they SLAM the blocks down and YELL every time they make a point. I'm, uh, getting where I can't think."

"I've made some calls. I'm getting a look at the DA's case."

"I need to get out of here so I can talk to people and see what's going down."

"That's difficult. Your bail is just so high."

"Isn't there any way you can get a judge to lower it? I'm not going anywhere. New Orleans is my home. I'm, like, planted here. They could put me under house arrest, couldn't they? I just need to get out of here."

"I'll keep trying."

"Okay, you're all I've got."

"Well, you've got your parents and lots of friends."

"My parents are too old to deal with this, and none of my friends have any money."

"I understand the problem, but the cops, you know, caught you with the stuff."

"It was a setup."

"Even so."

"Help me. Whatever you can do." The prisoner caught himself and made himself sound tough again. "I'll be all right. Gotta go. Other guys need to use the phone."

Tubby hung up slowly.

He checked his file and punched in the number for Judge Trapani's chambers.

"Just a minute, please. I'll see if he's in," a secretary said.

Tubby rehearsed the conversation in his mind.

Wonder if we might have lunch, Judge.

Why?

I see you're supporting Benny Bloom, and you know, I have to support Al Hughes publicly. I've known him a long time. But I want to make a really big contribution to you.

Yeah?

A great big one. I want to discuss it in private.

Okay.

Because there's this acquaintance of mine who's totally fucked unless you let him out of jail.

"Hello?" Judge Trapani was on the line.

Tubby slapped his hand over his mouth, afraid he might throw up, and slammed the phone into its cradle. He put his head down in his hands.

Clifford Banks's office expressed a musty elegance— old wood, old secretaries, old lawyers. Thus it took a few minutes for Banks's secretary to produce articles of incorporation for Mission Enterprises, chartering the company for "all lawful business purposes." Tubby and Marguerite were asked to bide their time in a conference room, alone with a carved mahogany table and twenty-four chairs. The Whiteside Bank Building, on whose seventh floor they were sitting, did not have modern amenities like picture windows, but it oozed the comforting feeling of being close to money.

Eventually Banks appeared with a handful of papers and took a seat.

"Sorry you had to wait," he said. "My secretary is

getting slower and slower since we made her switch to a computer. I think you'll find everything to be in order."

Tubby scanned the document. He and Banks were identified as the incorporators.

"Do you still have the sheriff's check?" Tubby asked.

"It's in my office," Banks said. "Quite safe."

"Here's our investment," Tubby said.

Marguerite handed over a bulky manila envelope full of diamonds and gold.

Banks peeked inside before quickly snapping it shut. He dropped it into an old leather briefcase.

"The sheriff told me what to expect," he said. "This will be picked up tomorrow, I'm told."

"Well, actually, since we're all friends here, it seems to me that since you've got our jewels we ought to hold the sheriff's check. Just for security, of course."

"It can't work that way. You could simply cash the check and run off with the money, though of course you wouldn't. I had better keep the check right in my office where it's perfectly safe. You've got to trust somebody some time, as they say. If for any reason the venture does not work out as planned, then everybody can get their money back."

"You win," Tubby said graciously. "It's all going to work out great. Frank knows a good deal when he sees one. It's time to start making big bucks."

Banks smiled. "Before we can start counting our gold, I need to review your prospectus. At first glance, it seems to me to be slightly thin on facts. And I must admit that I personally have never heard of Worldwide Women's Boxing."

Tubby was not worried about a cursory check of that organization. He had incorporated it in the State of Delaware two days ago. In time, of course, the dummy corporation would be seen for the paper front it really was. Tubby's original plan had been to siphon off the fake company's money for himself and his friends. When inevitably the scam was uncovered, he had hoped to so confuse the trail that Mulé would blame Clifford Banks, or even himself, for the final bankruptcy. But a new and more direct plan had formed in Tubby's mind as soon as he had seen Mulé's cashier's check payable to cash.

"The WWB is as real as it gets," he assured Banks. "Check on it all you want. But we need to get hopping because they are waiting to receive the first installment of the franchise fee . . ."

"Well, let me make a few calls. We should be able to get up and running in a day or two."

"No problem," Tubby said. Right now WWB's "headquarters" was an answering service, but that ought to suffice for the next twenty-four hours.

"I can promise you that we will make steady progress." Banks stared at Tubby.

"That's what I want," Tubby said enthusiastically. "Progress."

And fast, because it would not be long before Mulé realized that almost all of the jewels in the manila folder were artful fakes prepared by Tubby's client, Sandy Shandell, who had become a Mardi Gras artisan. While a few, like the gold bracelet the sheriff had so admired, were authentic, the rest of the real ones were concealed in a can of Café du Monde coffee in Tubby's kitchen. Marguerite had picked the hiding place herself.

Phase two of Tubby's new and more direct plan went into effect almost right away. A few hours following his departure from Banks's law firm, after night had fallen, Flowers entered the same building. He looked better than most of the maintenance staff in his green uniform. The patch on his pocket read JULIO. For props he carried an empty bucket and a mop. Simple is best, was his theory. On stakeouts, his favorite outfit was torn clothes, an empty quart bottle of beer, and a brown paper bag. With those symbols of homelessness you were completely unnoticeable—people avoided seeing you at all.

The security woman at the marble desk in the lobby of the Whiteside Bank Building started to say something when Flowers shuffled past, but she caught herself. Her job was to repel teenage boys during the day, and late at night, vagrants looking for a place to sleep. A man in a green uniform did not fit either profile.

The detective turned the corner to the wall of elevators and caught a car going up. He was humming "Remember When," a Victoria Cordova tune.

He exited at the seventh floor into a dark carpeted hallway facing a pair of heavy glass doors. The names of KEARNEY, COMEAUX, RAZPANTI & BANKS were etched in gold upon them. Flowers had an electronic device the size of a cigarette pack that caused the magnetic lock to pop open. He slid into a dark reception area. Guided by the knowledge that partners whose names are on the door occupy corner offices, Flowers set off in search for the one belonging to Clifford Banks.

It was not hard to find. The nameplate was illuminated by the glow from the adjoining office. Softly, Flowers crept toward the light and peered around the open doorway. An attorney in shirtsleeves was pecking away at his keyboard, his back turned.

Flowers withdrew and slipped into Banks's office as quietly as he could. The lights of the city glowed through the expansive windows, making navigation easy. Flowers sat behind Banks's desk in the attorney's soft leather chair and began opening drawers. The large one by his left ankle was locked. The detective picked it without difficulty. Expecting treasure, he was disappointed to find the drawer empty except for an unmarked videotape. Flowers thought it over for a second before sticking the tape inside his pocket and relocking the drawer.

There did not seem to be a wall safe hidden behind

any of the paintings of ducks, and Flowers was beginning to feel that his mission was to be a failure when he spied a leather briefcase under the hat rack by the door. It was not even locked, which was quite surprising since it was supposed to be loaded with Marguerite's imitation jewels. They were not there.

"Someone has already ripped us off," Flowers said to himself. In a zippered pocket, however, he found the cashier's check for five hundred thousand dollars. Who is this fool? he wondered to himself. Does he think a lawyer's office is invulnerable? The detective quickly swiped the check.

The lawyer next door was consoling his girlfriend on the telephone when Flowers made his getaway.

Exiting the elevators in the lobby, the detective almost bumped into the security guard who was prowling the halls. The woman told him to watch himself.

Outside the building an old man with worried eyes and gaps in his teeth asked Flowers for a buck. The detective paused long enough to give it to him.

"Thanks," the fellow said. "Us working guys gotta stick together."

29

The gala political rally was held on the eve of the election at the Ernest M. Morial Convention Center under the sponsorship of the Alliance for Reformed Government. It was a spectacular event, not to be missed by any of those who desired to sup at the trough of political patronage. All of the most prominent architects, engineers, and city planners were there, not to mention attorneys, purveyors of pens, pencils, and insurance, junior statesmen, and unemployed but multitalented people dreaming of political careers.

Waiting to greet them was the entire Alliance ticket, some forty munificent figures, anxious to fill vacancies from tax assessor to city councilwoman, in a hall that would comfortably seat two thousand.

As it was, only a portion of the hall, that right in front of the stage upon which the politicians were gathering, was reserved for sitters. Here were positioned the high rollers, in fat-waisted groups of eight, seated at round tables, enjoying cheese cubes, purple grapes, and wine for which they had paid five thousand dollars.

The rest of the vast room was open to the crowd of well-wishers who had plunked down a mere hundred dollars per ticket to stand and mingle. They could also drink wine for free or hit the cash bar. As individuals they occupied little space, on the average, and thus the hall could accommodate far more than two thousand in all.

A band known as the Thousand $ Car belted out homemade roots rock from a spot between the cash bars and contributed greatly to the overall gaiety and din.

All of the endorsed candidates were in attendance, together with their staffs, vital supporters, and most of the city's factual and impressionistic media. Some of the latter had arrived early to obtain good squatting positions up-front by the stage. They were liberally sampling the gratis offerings. A newspaper illustrator, already intoxicated by the atmosphere, cheerfully sketched a green olive that had escaped Sheriff Mulé's martini and rolled off the dais.

Tubby Dubonnet came to do his bit for Judge Al Hughes, one of the many stars of the show. Dressed to the nines, he steered his Chrysler to the front entrance, and while an attendant held the door for Marguerite

Patino, he tipped the valet parker twenty dollars to let the car stay where it was. The gesture impressed Marguerite and insured them an easy departure. Tubby had made dinner reservations an hour hence at Bayonna. He had had to twist an arm to get them and intended to keep his political hobnobbing on a tight schedule.

Even as they were locking up they could see Judge Hughes and his wife, Arabella, mount the steps and get swallowed by the crowd around the doors.

"Big turnout," Marguerite said. "This is a lot like Chicago."

Tubby flashed a pair of hundred-dollar tickets at the uniformed men standing on top of the steps, but security was very loose. The ARG idea was to build a boisterous crowd, not to keep anybody out.

Shaking hands and snagging two glasses of wine as he went, Tubby navigated Marguerite toward the shade of a tall rubber tree, which subtly marked the divide between standing room only and reserved seating. He waved at Al Hughes, who had now climbed up onto the stage. The judge beckoned him forward, but Tubby ignored the invitation.

"Gee," Marguerite said. "How would you even get a drink around here?" She was jostled from behind by a large woman trying to get her photograph taken with a television newsman.

"At your service." Tubby handed her one of his plastic glasses of wine. "After this you're on your own."

The program was beginning.

Alphonse D'Amica, president of ARG, took center stage in the midst of his candidates and began speaking unintelligibly through a screeching microphone.

Clifford Banks tapped Tubby on the shoulder, mouthed a chilling hello, and moved on.

After some mechanical adjustments, D'Amica's voice thundered throughout the hall, summoning the entire field of endorsed candidates for public office to come to the stage for public viewing. Nimble Vietnamese waiters swirled around among the tables.

At that moment, Daisy was being dropped off across the street by a White Cloud cab. She was nervous, and was hurrying toward the convention center when she heard the taxi driver yelling that she owed him eight fifty. She had to run back to pay.

She approached the busy building cautiously, concealing herself behind a cluster of peanut vendors until she got close. The security guards at the entrance, however, were yakking it up with a chubby man sporting a pie-sized SAM ARUBA FOR CONSTABLE button, and she made it inside without a problem.

Weaving her way through the crowd, she saw Tubby by a rubber tree and changed her route to avoid him.

"Here they all are. The selected few. The leaders of our community now and for tomorrow," D'Amica bellowed into the microphone.

"Get to know your candidates," he screamed as the supportive throng jockeyed for position, and flashbulbs started popping.

Daisy grabbed a drink from a passing tray and

pushed up to the front. At the center of the stage, Al Hughes was posing for a picture, theatrically shaking hands with Sheriff Frank Mulé.

Mulé saw Tubby in the crowd and waved at him. A gleam of gold flashed on his wrist. The sheriff pointed to the bracelet he had swiped from Marguerite's loot and bared his teeth in a wicked laugh.

Tubby reached inside his coat a pulled out a yellow certified check for five hundred thousand dollars. He held it daintily between thumb and forefinger and waved it aloft for the sheriff to see. Mulé stared at what was in Tubby's hand, and his eyes darkened.

Daisy was standing on one leg trying to get her pistol out of her garter when she was almost knocked off balance by a bump from behind.

"Excuse me, ma'am," an ebony-skinned college boy apologized. "They pushed me."

Three Vietnamese waiters converged on the stage. Each drew a revolver from his vest. Oblivious, Daisy raised her own little gun and pointed it with both hands.

The sheriff saw her first and made a grab for the judge, thinking to use him as a shield. Hughes, however, refused the role.

"Get back, Sheriff," he cried. "She wants you, not me." He shoved Mulé away with such conviction that the sheriff almost fell off the stage and onto the woman below.

He was caught in midfall by blasts from the waiters' arsenal.

In the excitement, Daisy fired twice. Mulé buckled from repeated hits. He spun around and collapsed on the floor, spurting blood.

Surprised by the ease of her attack, Daisy stared transfixed for a moment as pandemonium erupted all around her. She turned to go and again confronted the young man.

"Dude," he said, awestruck, and stood aside to let her pass.

Panic had seized the audience, and there was a mad scramble for the exits. The waiters jumped onto the stage, leapt over the huddled politicians, and ran out the back. Daisy pushed her way to the front exits with the rest of the people.

She didn't hear Alphonse D'Amica call for a doctor. She did not see, or else she might have commenced another battle, Willie LaRue snaking through the throng in pursuit. She felt, however, a hand grab her shoulder just as she reached the main gateway. Swinging around, ready to fight, she found that it was Tubby who was restraining her. He pushed her in the direction of a baby-blue Le Baron parked at curbside.

"Get in, get in!" he kept shouting.

Dazed, she did as directed and stumbled into the passenger seat. Tubby ran around to the driver's side and Marguerite, hurrying to keep up, leapt into the back.

With the help of its authoritative horn, the big Chrysler parted the sea of people departing the convention center and broke free down the freshly paved street. A string of police cars and ambulances shot past, going in the opposite direction.

"What are we doing?" Marguerite shrieked from the backseat.

"Don't ask me any questions yet. I'm still figuring things out," Tubby yelled. "Daisy, don't say a thing until I tell you to." He need not have issued that order. But for rocking with the motion of the car, Daisy was sitting motionless and staring out the window with a slight smile on her lips.

"Goddamn, you plugged him," Tubby said, twisting the wheel and shooting up Poydras Street. "Don't say anything," he repeated.

Marguerite realized that neither Tubby nor Daisy had seen the three gunmen.

"I could get disbarred for this," Tubby said out loud.

A car cut them off at Baronne Street.

"Watch where you're going!" Tubby yelled, careening across two lanes and then continuing on. He was quite agitated.

"Jesus, I wonder how many people in that hall can identify you?" Tubby said excitedly. "Or me! How many can identify me driving you away?"

"I didn't see what happened," Marguerite said, perversely intrigued by Tubby's agitation. "Did this woman shoot the sheriff?"

"No, no. You didn't see anything? Of course not. I didn't actually see it myself. Not exactly. There was a lot of commotion. It was hard to see what was going on." He was speeding past the Superdome. The lights stretched green all the way to Broad.

"Got the son of a bitch," Daisy said proudly. She was beginning to shake.

"I told you not to talk yet," Tubby shouted. "You're overwhelmed and overcome. We'll all go someplace quiet. Where it's safe. Of course, if an arrest warrant is issued for you, I'll have to advise you to turn yourself in. As a lawyer to a client, of course." The Model Rules of Ethics were flashing through his mind, and he mentally slashed whole sections away searching for slender principles that might excuse his actions.

"None of us are witnesses, after all," he said more calmly. The Le Baron was approaching Fountainbleau, where the trees were thicker and the houses bigger. Daisy laid her head back on the seat and closed her eyes. She was well pleased.

"The important thing is to find a safe place."

Tubby had concluded his internal dialogue, and he softened the pressure of his toe on the accelerator.

He pulled to the curb beside a towering palmetto and cut the engine.

"Where are we and why are you helping me?" Daisy asked in a dreamy voice.

Tubby ignored her.

"Whatever the woman may have done," he explained to Marguerite, "is entirely justified in my mind. Her greatest peril, however, is not the police or the law, but a legion of psychotic killers like LaRue who undoubtedly are at this moment searching for her. She has to get out of town, for her own safety. Any ideas?"

"Sure," Marguerite said. "I could take her on a trip. I'm thinking Santa Fe."

Tubby nodded. "It could just be a short trip. Then you could come back."

"Or you could come for me. You need a vacation." She smiled.

"Yeah. Well, I'll be working on that. I should probably take you straight to the airport."

"I'm not going anywhere without Charlie's belt buckle," Daisy interrupted from the backseat.

"What are you talking about?" Tubby demanded.

"Charlie. His father gave me Charlie's silver Harley-Davidson belt buckle because he knew how he cared for me. It's in my room, and I ain't going anywhere without it."

"Where's your room?"

"On Airline Highway. It's called the Tomcat Inn."

"Okay. I know where that is. It's on the way." He turned the key and the motor purred.

"You know where that is?" Marguerite asked sweetly.

30

LaRue saw Tubby drive the two women away. His own car was in the public garage, however, and he had no realistic hope of following. Instead he worked his way back into the hall to ascertain the condition of his employer.

He watched as a doctor, apparently a guest of the party, attended to Mulé, while Alphonse D'Amica shooed the curious away. There was a wet pool of blood around the sheriff's head. A strange man was pointing at the sheriff's limp wrist. "That's my bracelet," he kept insisting. A squad of paramedics came running across the emptying floor, pulling a stretcher and lugging some equipment. After a short parlay they bundled Mulé up, strapped him to the gurney, and stuck an oxygen mask on his face.

" 'Fraid he's dead," the doctor said to the EMT before they wheeled the sheriff away.

"Best leave that to the hospital," the medic replied.

The rest of the politicians had exited or returned to the bars, where fairly large numbers of voters still were congregated.

LaRue grabbed a handful of mushroom caps stuffed with Parmesan cheese from a plate left on a now-empty table and pondered his next move.

He had seen what Tubby had pulled from his pocket, and it looked very much like a five hundred thousand dollar check payable to cash. One of the fugitives, he figured, might also be forced to hand over a fortune in jewels.

LaRue set off in pursuit of the three conspirators.

All three of them, the tourist, the assassin, and the attorney, cruised at high speed down the dark straight highway pointed west. They had been delayed briefly by Marguerite's insistence that she be permitted to gather a few of her personal belongings for the trip, which meant a detour to Tubby's house. True to her word, she had packed and gotten out the door in less than ten minutes, but it was precious time lost.

Tubby barely braked as he approached the gap-toothed neon sign advertising THE TOMCAT INN—BEST

RATES ON AIRLINE. He swerved into the driveway. The Le Baron bounced hard over the speed bumps and ran to the curb.

"I'll be right back," Daisy promised and scampered out of the car.

"Do you want me to come with you?" Marguerite called after her, and Daisy yelled no. Tubby left the motor running, ready for a quick getaway.

"There's a ten o'clock flight to Houston," he told Marguerite. "From there you can get to just about anyplace."

"We haven't had much time together, but I'll have to admit it hasn't been dull." She poked his stomach.

"It's been, uh, nice having you here," Tubby admitted. Marguerite took his hand. Tubby was such a sweet man. Some day she would have to straighten him out. They didn't notice a blue Ford enter the parking lot and cut its lights. It halted by the office, fifty feet away.

"Are you going to miss me?" she asked.

"You know, Marguerite . . ." He didn't get to finish.

The door of Daisy's room swung open and she came out, clutching a small bag. When she spotted LaRue trotting across the parking lot she brought the bag to her breast and screamed.

Tubby saw his enemy, gun in hand, in his rearview mirror and reacted automatically. He crammed the shifter into reverse and mashed the gas pedal. Tires squealing, the Le Baron accelerated backward.

The bumper caught LaRue right below the belt and bowled him over. With hardly a murmur, the big car

rolled over the surprised man and crashed into the side
of LaRue's car. The Chrysler's trunk lid flew open.

Tubby screamed at Daisy, and she ran for the car to
jump in.

Tubby put the car into gear and drove over the man
again. This time, both of the tires thumped.

He mashed the gas pedal and peeled out of the parking lot. A forgotten plastic box in the truck had been
knocked open by the collision, and as the car accelerated a cloud of ashes blew from the back. Spinning in
the air, the dust formed fairy faces, had anyone been
there to see them. Some were recognizable, some were
a mystery. They drifted around the parking lot and settled over LaRue's crumpled body. In Tubby's mind a
row of corpses appeared and just as quickly vanished.

Neither the driver nor his passengers had anything to
say to each other until they were almost to Moisant
Field.

"Now I finally know what they mean by justice,"
Daisy said at last, almost to herself.

"I wonder if any judge would agree with you,"
Tubby replied. His mind had entered a new zone.

"I don't really care what any of your judges would
say. Last one I met was too busy trying to get his pecker
out of his pants to care about who's breaking the law."

"You can't justify what you did and I did that easily,"
Tubby said.

"Candy-ass Trapani," she muttered, watching the
flicker of the approaching runway lights.

Tubby shot her a quick look.

"Who?" he said finally.

"Candy-ass Trapani. He was my date at Benny Bloom's hotel room."

Tubby drove in silence.

"Talk about a distinguishing characteristic," Daisy said.

"What was it?" Marguerite asked, turning around.

"I can't believe this crap," Tubby said.

He followed the signs to departing flights.

"Why don't you just whisper it in my ear," he suggested.

Daisy did, right before the car reached the curb.

Later, heading home, the thought crossed the lawyer's mind that Cesar Pitillero's chances for early release on his cocaine charge had dramatically improved.

31

On Saturday morning, election day, campaign signs sprouted like poppies on the neutral grounds of Orleans Parish, and Tubby slept late. When he finally roused himself and cleared his head sufficiently to retrieve the newspaper from the front sidewalk, the headline told him that Sheriff Frank Mulé was dead.

He had been struck by bullets from three different guns in what was being termed a gangland-type slaying. This did not make much sense. The deceased had been wearing a bracelet that a witness at the scene identified as having come from a robbery at First Alluvial Bank.

Tubby was sipping a shot of coffee and chicory when he got a phone call from Clifford Banks.

"We've got a few problems to work out," Banks said.

"Like what?" Tubby asked. He was afraid Banks might be ready to accuse him of murder.

"Like the theft of an item from my office."

"I don't know anything about that," Tubby said with relief.

"I insist that we meet."

Though tempted to hang up the phone, he acquiesced. They picked a time early in the afternoon. Neither lawyer favored an office visit, and they settled upon a walk in Audubon Park, along the Mississippi River.

Banks was sitting on a bench watching the oil tankers battle the current when Tubby arrived. The bond attorney, wearing a tie and cradling a leather briefcase, was easy to spot by the sole practitioner in baggy khaki trousers.

"You didn't need to dress up," Tubby said.

"It's my standard uniform," Banks said. "I'm used to it, you know."

Tubby sat down on the bench.

"I am making the assumption that you have our five hundred thousand dollar check," Banks said.

"If I do, I'd say it's as much mine as anybody's." Tubby stared at the current.

"Why?" Banks asked. "Just because Mulé is gone?"

"That's right," Tubby said. "The king is dead. To the victor belongs the spoils."

"Be serious," Banks said. "Business is business. You think we liquidate just because of an unexpected downsizing?"

"Well, sure," Tubby replied in surprise. "Frank was the boss, wasn't he, the big cheese, the guy at the top? He was responsible for all the deals."

"Nonsense," Banks said. "We will all miss Frank, of course. He was an important person and often handy to have around, if intellect wasn't required, but the team goes on."

"The team?" Tubby asked. "Sheriff Mulé was not the crime czar?"

"That's a very odd term," Banks said disapprovingly. "I don't know what you're talking about. This is a business. It's not dependent on any one man, and certainly not on a czar."

"And you? Are you the chairman of the board?"

Banks smiled thinly. "It would be more accurate to say that I am the attorney for a number of serious businessmen who rely upon me to protect their interests, but no. There is no permanent chairman of the board."

"Damn." Tubby watched a seagull peck at a pile of fish heads somebody had deposited on the sidewalk.

"We wish to go ahead with the project," Banks continued, interrupting Tubby's reverie.

"My deal was with Frank Mulé," Tubby said. "I don't really know you."

"We'll get to know each other better," Banks assured him.

Improvisation is critical to success, a law professor had once taught him.

"If that's the way you want it," Tubby said, scratching his head, "you'll have to act immediately. The funds to pay for the WWB franchise must be delivered to New York by tomorrow at the latest. That's the deadline I've been given. I have other investors lined up ready to move if you're not," Tubby lied. "If your team wants in, it's got to be now."

"But I haven't been able to fully investigate Worldwide Women's Boxing." Banks hesitated. "There hasn't been sufficient time."

"You have all the figures. You've got my jewels as collateral. You know the profit potential of the franchise. You'll have to fish or cut bait. That's all there is to it. Let's pretend that the check for five hundred thousand is in my pocket right now. If you'll endorse the back of it, so I know it's your money, not Mulé's, I'll send it off today. That will hold them until you can convert my stuff into cash."

"I'm not sure where your jewels are at present," Banks reflected, almost to himself. "Frank got them and they haven't been seen since." He rubbed his smooth chin. "Okay," he said finally. "I guess you have to trust somebody sometime. Besides, you'd have to be a very naive individual to think you could get way with cheating us."

That's me, naive, Tubby thought as he watched Banks sign his name to the back of the check. Now where would the trail point when the team's bloodhounds came sniffing? He folded the yellow paper carefully, and stuck it in his wallet.

"I'll see that it gets delivered," Tubby said.

Banks's brow was furrowed as he watched his new

partner drive away. He would have to commence a thorough scrutiny of Worldwide Women's Boxing right away.

Tubby went directly to his office. He was fully aware that Banks, not being as easily distracted by sweaty muscular females as the sheriff had been, would soon expose his dummy boxing corporation. Tubby pressed his lips to the check and kissed it good-bye. To keep it was to go to jail, and his price for such a dishonor was higher than half a million bucks. Instead, he addressed a plain white envelope to Bureau of Finance, City of New Orleans. He put a yellow sticker on the check and wrote on it, as anonymously as possible, "Here's my contribution to the City's general fund. Keep up the good work."

Based upon his experiences with City Hall, odds were good that whichever lowly paid civil servant opened the envelope would either boost the check or would deposit it into the city treasury without further inquiry. In either case, the money might possibly do some good.

And in either case, Banks would have a hell of a time getting it back. Tubby had once overpaid his occupational license fee and it had taken three years to get his ninety-eight-dollar refund. Clifford's own backers might not be that patient.

Walking away from the mailbox on the corner, Tubby wondered whether he ought not take an extended trip.

Cherrylynn could run the office while he was away.

For finances he had all of Marguerite's jewels.

For the rest of today, however, he was going home and catch some rest—maybe watch some college football games on television—anything but watch the election news.

Tulane was beating LSU 40 to 3 in the fourth quarter when the real world intruded. Tubby tried to ignore the telephone, but it wouldn't stop ringing. Finally, thinking it might be a family emergency, he reached for the handset. He regretted it at once.

"Hey, Mr. Tubby, it's me, Monster Mudbug."

"Yes, Adrian, what's the problem now?"

"No problem at all, Mr. Tubby. I just got elected sheriff. It's because Sheriff Mulé got shot. I got more than two hundred votes."

Tubby set the phone down on the couch pillow and started laughing.

"Can you believe that, Mr. Tubby?" he heard the Monster crowing. "Tell me what I'm supposed to do now?"

"Free the captives," Tubby wheezed into the phone. "That's what the good book says."

"I know you're kidding, Mr. Tubby. Listen, do you know where that girl Daisy went to? We kind of hit it off right after your party, and I'd really like to find her."

"I don't know what to tell you, Adrian. If I talk to her, I'll let her know about your interest, but I gotta warn you. She kisses for keeps."

．　．　．

On the Southwest flight to Santa Fe, Marguerite and Daisy relaxed with little green bottles of California Chardonnay.

"I've never been so far west before," Daisy said, looking at the sky full of stars outside the plane's window.

"Could be the beginning of a brand-new life for you," Marguerite said, smiling faintly.

"Oh, I don't think so. You have to live your same life anywhere you go. And I won't have a job or much of anything else right away."

"I'll help you get settled in." Marguerite sipped from her plastic cup. "Then we'll just have to see what happens."

"I just want some time off without hassles," Daisy said. "You know what I mean? And no heavy love affairs. I just lose my grip when I fall in love."

"It's hard for a woman to maintain her identity in a man's world," Marguerite said.

"Where's all the so-called men?"

"Everywhere you look."

"Nowhere I looked, except for Charlie. You don't like Tubby?"

"I'll answer that when we get to know each other better."

"I try to keep my eyes open for the good things in life that are supposed to be free, but there's always this money thing."

"Right now money is the least of our worries." Marguerite patted the lumpy purse that rested heavily in her lap. "And I think your sentiments are just fine. We're going to get along okay."

Tubby wanted to get a closer look at his treasure—to experience in solitude the feel of diamonds and gold running through his fingers. He went to the pantry for the coffee can where Marguerite and he had secreted the jewels, but as soon as he lifted it from the shelf he knew there was a problem. The can was empty but for a note.

"You will always be my dreamer," it said. "Love, Marguerite."

A little later, Tubby called Al Hughes at home to congratulate him on his reelection victory.

"Your good wishes are appreciated, Counselor, but I'll have to be honest. I don't think I'm going to ask you to be chairman of any more of my campaigns."

"Once was enough for me, too, Al. You just go out there and be a good judge, and I'll be happy."

"There was never any question about that," Hughes said firmly. "And there ain't going to be."

"You swamped Benny Bloom."

"Shows the voters aren't always stupid."

"I never did understand why he wanted the job anyway."

"My sources say he handled payoffs for certain of my colleagues on the bench. He wanted to eliminate the middleman and get the money himself."

"What?" Tubby asked in astonishment. "Other than maybe Trapani, there are other judges taking payoffs to fix cases?"

"Yes, according to our reporter friend Kathy Jeansonne. I'm not going to talk about it on the telephone."

"But you're going to report it to someone?"

"I'm going to do something, but I'm not prepared to say what. First, I'm going to wait and see if the shooting has stopped. This is a scary time to be a politician."

"Just take care of yourself."

"That's Mrs. Hughes's job. Mine is to wear the robe."

The ghoulish visitors that had troubled Tubby's slumbers did not visit him that night. Not even LaRue came to call. The sleeper sensed that they were gone. In their place came more pleasant images of people still warm with life. His attention, focused for too long on the dead and undeserving, returned now to the living. He breathed easily and woke up with an appetite.

• • • •

It was blue skies, cool, and sunny over the Rigolets in the early morning. Two fishermen reclining in chairs at either end of a fourteen-foot fiberglass skiff cast lazily at the tall grass along the marshy shore. Mesmerized by the tiny waves rolling past the clear thread of his fishing line, Tubby Dubonnet whistled a tune.

"You're going to scare the specks," Raisin called from the front of the boat.

"I don't think there are any fish around here, anyway." The thought did not bother Tubby. He had not shaved that morning, and the hair under his hat was unbrushed. He felt good.

There had been no mention in the newspaper about the death of Willie LaRue. Running over the maniac had been an act of self-defense, Tubby was pretty sure of that. Still, this was the one part of the story that he had not shared with anyone, not even Raisin.

"I think I'm going to cut back on the booze," Tubby announced.

"That's a damn good idea," Raisin said. "How about tossing me a beer."

Tubby leaned over to the ice chest and dredged out a silver can. He tossed it to his partner, who deftly snagged it with one hand, and he opened another for himself.

"I feel like I've just been lost in a thick fog for the past six months. Now I'm ready to get back into the world again."

"No more talk about the crime czar?"

"It's a committee. How can you fight a committee? A group of nameless individuals, not one of whom has the guts to be the baddest guy in town? They're not worth my time."

"Whatever you say." Raisin twitched his pole left and right and gently reeled in his line.

"It's like my daughter said, 'Daddy, it's time you got a life.'"

"Seems to me you might worry about what the committee's going to do to you," Raisin said.

"I doubt they'll come after me," Tubby said, more bravely than he felt. If they did, he would just have to take his chances. "Committees don't feel human emotions like revenge. Now, Frank Mulé would have burned me alive. He was a man with emotions. I think the board of directors will look at the bottom line and see there's no profit in messing with me." They might have enough to worry about with Bin Minny on the loose.

"You're just a small fry."

"Exactly. Of course they might demote Clifford Banks."

"So what's next?"

"I plan to get my law practice back together and start spending some more time with my girls and my new grandbaby."

"Just lead the straight life."

"That's right."

A white egret circled the boat and landed in the marsh grass a hundred yards away. It stood tall on one leg and pointed its beak at the fishermen, eyes searching for bait.

"Have you had the chance to look at that videotape your detective swiped from Clifford Banks's office yet?"

"Can't say as I have."

"It'd give us something to do when we get home," Raisin suggested.

"No, man, we're going to be frying fish," Tubby said with confidence. His line went taut and his rod bowed. The egret's beak twitched, imagining lunch.

Match wits with the bestselling
MYSTERY WRITERS
in the business!

SARA PARETSKY
"Paretsky's name always makes the top of the list when people talk about the new female operatives." —The New York Times Book Review

- [ ] **BLOOD SHOT** 20420-8 $6.99
- [ ] **BURN MARKS** 20845-9 $6.99
- [ ] **INDEMNITY ONLY** 21069-0 $6.99
- [ ] **GUARDIAN ANGEL** 21399-1 $6.99
- [ ] **KILLING ORDERS** 21528-5 $6.99
- [ ] **DEADLOCK** 21332-0 $6.99
- [ ] **TUNNEL VISION** 21752-0 $6.99
- [ ] **WINDY CITY BLUES** 21873-X $6.99
- [ ] **A WOMAN'S EYE** 21335-5 $6.99
- [ ] **WOMEN ON THE CASE** 22325-3 $6.99

HARLAN COBEN
Winner of the Edgar, the Anthony, and the Shamus Awards

- [ ] **DEAL BREAKER** 22044-0 $5.50
- [ ] **DROP SHOT** 22049-5 $5.50
- [ ] **FADE AWAY** 22268-0 $5.50
- [ ] **BACK SPIN** 22270-2 $5.50

RUTH RENDELL
"There is no finer mystery writer than Ruth Rendell." —San Diego Union Tribune

- [ ] **THE CROCODILE BIND** 21865-9 $5.99
- [ ] **SIMISOLA** 22202-8 $5.99
- [ ] **KEYS TO THE STREET** 22392-X $5.99

LINDA BARNES

- [ ] **COYOTE** 21089-5 $5.99
- [ ] **STEEL GUITAR** 21268-5 $5.99
- [ ] **BITTER FINISH** 21606-0 $4.99
- [ ] **SNAPSHOT** 21220-0 $5.99
- [ ] **CITIES OF THE DEAD** 22095-5 $5.50
- [ ] **DEAD HEAT** 21862-4 $5.50
- [ ] **HARDWARE** 21223-5 $5.99

At your local bookstore or use this handy page for ordering:
DELL READERS SERVICE, DEPT. DIS
2451 South Wolf Road, Des Plaines, IL . 60018
Please send me the above title(s). I am enclosing $_____
(Please add $2.50 per order to cover shipping and handling.) Send check or money order—no cash or C.O.D.s please.

Dell

Ms./Mrs./Mr. _____

Address _____

City/State _____ Zip _____

DGM-12/97

Prices and availability subject to change without notice. Please allow four to six weeks for delivery.